Mike

Harlequin Presents..

Other titles by

ANNE HAMPSON
IN HARLEQUIN PRESENTS

ANNE HAMPSON

a kiss from satan

HARLEQUIN BOOKS
toronto-winnipeg

Original hard cover edition published in 1973
by Mills & Boon Limited.

SBN 373-70513-1
Harlequin Presents edition published July 1973

Printed in Canada.

CHAPTER ONE

THE gardens of Lime Cottage, a rambling old house of character set amid three acres of matured woodland, were subtly illuminated by lamps fixed under the eaves and by fairy lights hung in the trees. All along one edge of the wide sweeping lawn a thick belt of Scots pines towered to the dark sky; under these trees charcoal fires burned brightly and eager helpers cooked lamb cutlets and sausages and joints of chicken.

The barbecue was being held in place of the customary Senate dinner, and in addition to the members of the Senate, numerous other guests had been invited, bringing the total up to over a hundred. Gale Davis was there, her father being a lecturer at the university; Tricia Sims was there, looking deliriously happy because she was shortly to be married to Trevis Chard, who at present was with his uncle in Birmingham, learning the business of running a chain of supermarkets which he would one day inherit. Although Gale and Tricia were friends, Gale had not yet met Travis, and it now seemed she would not do so until the wedding. Also present at the barbecue was Julius Spiridon, here at the invitation of Professor Ingham, whose friend he had been since their student days. Julius, whose business was in tourism, made frequent visits to Britain and naturally he stayed with his old friend. At thirty-five he was still a bachelor – which was unusual for a Greek – and this was not the first occasion on which Gale had permitted herself a secret smile on beholding the admiring and hopeful glances of all the single women present. Tall and slim, with iron-grey hair, thick and slightly waved over a low and furrowed brow, Julius Spiridon was the most distinguished-looking man present at any function he happened to attend. Attractive he most certainly was, Gale had to admit, but the dark granite features, coupled with eyes as dark and hard as basalt itself, spelled a formidable personality, an inflexibility and complete lack of feeling. Gale was sure the man possessed a ruthlessness that was permanent and deep. Heaven help the woman who eventually married him, Gale had said to herself the moment she was introduced to him at a party a few months previously. He had returned to his own country a short while later, to his home on the lovely Aegean island of Patmos where he owned a large and ultra-modern blue and white villa with magnificent views to the sea, so Gale had not been afforded an opportunity of widening her knowledge about him.

He was dancing with Gale's friend, Deborah Curtis, while Gale herself danced with her own brother who had come down from the north of England a few days previously, mainly to see his mother but also because of the invitation he had received to attend the barbecue. Watching Deborah, Gale had to smile. Poor Deb, who had fallen for the cold Greek despite the assurance of several well-meaning friends that, if Julius had any interest in women at all, it would be merely bound up in their transient value as diversions, slipped in hurriedly between his business duties.

'What are you playing at with Robert Coles?' Her brother's voice brought Gale back from her interest in her friend and she glanced up at him from under incredibly long dark eyelashes.

'Breaking his heart, I hope,' she replied coolly, her

eyes glinting suddenly.

'You fool, Gale!'

She laughed, and Edward frowned. For it was an ugly laugh that clashed harshly with the soft beauty of her face.

'Not at all. I'm enjoying myself.'

'Must you go on – taking it out of every other man just because of what Malcolm did to you?'

'It isn't only because of Malcolm; it's my own private war on all men because none of them are any good.'

'That's a sweeping statement, and a damned stupid and unthinking one. Am I rotten, then?'

'Not yet. But it wouldn't surprise me in the least if you were to prove unfaithful to Anthea some time in the future.'

'Thanks.' Edward's voice was clipped. 'You're a cynic, Gale, and a not very attractive one at that!'

She gave a small sigh, but the hardness in her eyes remained.

'At eighteen I was a little softie – trusting and—'

'Very sweet,' came the swift interruption. 'Now, at twenty-three, you're a tough and thoroughly unlikeable young woman.'

'Thank *you*, Edward,' with a hint of tartness. 'But other men don't appear to think so.'

'Other men who have not been attacked.'

'Attacked? What a unique way of putting it!'

'What sort of satisfaction do you derive from making men fall in love with you and then throwing them over?'

'A great deal of satisfaction – and you needn't look like that, Edward, all sorry for them, because if a woman doesn't hurt a man then you can be sure he'll hurt her. Look at Father, and the life Mother's had with him. Look at him now – over there, flirting as usual. No wonder Mother prefers to stay at home; she naturally doesn't want to sit and watch her husband giving all his attention to another woman, as Father invariably does. Just think of her, all on her own at home – reading a book or something.'

'We both offered to stay in with her,' reminded Edward. 'But she wouldn't hear of it.'

'Simply because she can't bear to spoil other people's pleasure. You don't for one moment believe she prefers to be alone, do you?'

'She should have put her foot down long ago. Father wouldn't be like this if she'd done so.'

'Rubbish! Father's a profligate and you know it. One woman isn't enough for him – or for any man, it would seem.'

'Thinking of Malcolm again,' he stated on a note of irritation. 'All right, he was unfaithful while being engaged to you, but you can't put every other man on his level.'

'What about Josie – my friend – who's been married less than a year, and Mark running off with another girl? Don't defend your sex, Edward. Be honest and admit they're untrustworthy to a man.'

A deep sigh escaped him; he changed the subject abruptly, plainly anxious not to quarrel with his sister.

'Our Greek friend seems to be affected by your beauty; he hasn't taken his eyes off you the whole evening.'

'Indeed? I hadn't noticed.' But she had . . . and it annoyed her to admit to being affected by this attention. Not once since the break with Malcolm five years ago had any man been able to arouse either her interest or her emotions. During the process of retaliation she had acquired an immunity – or so she had firmly believed. But the Greek was devastatingly masculine; he wore that particular air of authority that thrilled a woman even while she owned that it could very well lead to complete subjugation, since this was the Greek tradition. Man was master, woman his subordinate.

'He's also attracting as much feminine attention as ever,' said Edward, ignoring her comment.

'More than is good for his vanity,' retorted Gale with an edge of contempt to her voice. 'He could do with a set-down!'

Edward laughed suddenly and said, eyeing his sister with a curious expression,

'You're not going to try anything out on him, I hope?' Gale made no answer, because she was thoughtfully watching Julius, whose expression was one of faint contempt as he glanced down into the starry eyes of his partner. There was no doubt that his opinion of women in general was low in the extreme. How inordinately satisfying it would be to have him fall in love . . . and then callously throw him over! 'Julius Spiridon's a very different kettle of fish from all those others whose hearts you've set out to break,' Edward was continuing. 'I advise you to have a care, Gale.'

Her attractively-arched brows lifted a fraction and a smile hovered on her lips.

'I can take care of myself,' she told him confidently. 'Perhaps you're right about his being different from the rest, though,' she went on to concede. And then she added, as if forced to do so, 'It would be fun to try out my charms on him all the same. He might just fall – it's possible, I'm sure.'

'One of these days,' returned Edward not without a hint of malice, 'you're going to meet your match!'

'It's five years since Malcolm let me down,' she reminded him with a subtle inflection which he was swift to discern.

'You're telling me you've escaped mishaps up till now? Well, that doesn't signify that you can continue for ever. I don't know whether or not you're serious about having fun with our Greek,' he went on, 'but if you take my advice you'll drop the idea. He's far too formidable; he'll never go under in any battle, especially one involving a woman.'

'Thanks for the warning, but it isn't necessary. I can take care of myself.'

'You're altogether too confident,' he almost snapped, swinging Gale towards the belt of pines where people were eating round the fires. 'You're also too proud of your achievements – and pride goes before a fall, remember.

Gale only laughed, a harsh laugh that brought another frown to her brother's brow. His thoughts were not difficult to read. This was not the sister of their childhood. How could a girl so naïve and gentle at the age of eighteen become the hard and cynical woman she was now, at twenty-three? That was what he was asking himself, and Gale bit her lip. Sometimes she herself regretted the change, wished she had not allowed herself to be affected in the way she had been affected, desiring only revenge, wanting only to see other men suffer. And they had suffered. There had been Stephen, who had fallen madly in love with her, as she had meant him to. She threw him over, immune to his pleadings. But his hurt could not have gone all that deep, for he was now married and he and his wife were expecting their first child. Then there was Michael, who actually threatened to do himself an injury. That had frightened her at the time and she had not bothered with anyone else for over a year. However, Michael was also married – which only went to prove that men never loved really deeply. Nevertheless, Gale still enjoyed making them suffer, even though the suffering was only temporary.

Her eyes wandered once more to the tall arresting Greek. Yes, it would certainly be fun. . . .

'I've warned you.' Edward's voice, clear and precise, as he followed the direction of her gaze and seemed to guess what her thoughts were. 'He isn't only a charmer, he's also a seducer – if gossip has any foundation – and it usually does have.'

'If I do decide to – er – work on him,' laughed Gale, 'I promise I'll take care. I'll make sure I don't find myself in a vulnerable position.'

'And what do you term a vulnerable position?' dryly from her brother as she stopped dancing and, taking her arm, led her over to where the food was being served.

'The sort of position which might prove to be dangerous. He can scarcely seduce me in a crowd.'

'I agree. But neither can you do very much in a crowd. If you're bent on mischief you'll have to be alone with him at times.'

Gale said nothing, simply because she was herself beginning to see the impossibility of even becoming friendly with a man whose visits to England were of such short duration. The opportunities of meeting him occurred only when there was an occasion such as this, and so the idea faded out almost as soon as it was born.

But a short while later Gale found herself seething, and once again wishing she could give the arrogant Greek the set-down he deserved. She had wandered off alone in the grounds, away from the crowd and the dancing and the smell of food frying or being turned on the spit. She found a seat in a little arbour at the end of a lonely path, and sat down, unaware, for the moment, that Julius and his friend were seated on the other side of the rose-hedge. Then she heard their voices, plainly, and edged with laughter. They were talking about women.

'So completely without strength of character,' Professor Ingham was saying. 'Frivolous in the extreme – and so very easy to conquer.'

'I agree – boringly easy. I'd prefer a fight myself, but place your hand on a woman's heart and she's yours instantly.'

The two men laughed again, and Gale's temper was such that the blood fairly pounded in her head. Never had she been in such a rage. 'Place your hand on a woman's heart and she's yours instantly.' What a hateful, arrogant and pompous creature! He ought to be tortured – slowly!

Almost suffocated by her fury, Gale rose from her seat and silently made her way back to the music and the lights. Half an hour later Julius asked her to dance; she slid into his arms, but in a moment or two the waltz ended and they were dancing face to face but apart. She glanced up at him, fluttering her lashes and recalling what Edward had said about Julius being affected by her and not being able to take his eyes off her. If he were only slightly interested it was a good start, she thought, smiling her most charming smile and even herself being totally unaware of just how adorable she looked. The hardness no longer marred her features. the lovely contours of her face were clear and finely sculptured; her eyes were wide and innocent, her mouth quivering as if inviting a kiss. Julius's own eyes kindled strangely; she noted a movement in his throat as he continued to look into her face. And then his gaze wandered – to the lovely arch of her neck, and the pale gold hair falling to her shoulders. His eyes roved her curves and she felt a hint of colour rise. He smiled faintly on noting this and, even though the music had not changed, he drew her into his arms and they danced away from everyone else, ending up a long way off, under a great spreading oak where all was dark but for the sprays of moonlight filtering through the branches of the tree.

The music was faintly heard still, but suddenly it stopped. Julius retained his hold and Gale became intensely aware of the hardness of his body against hers, the gentle caressing movement of his hands as they came round from her back to settle on her waist. The moment was fraught with tension, no words being spoken, and with only the rustle of leaves to break the hush of night. Julius's hands moved again and Gale averted her head, unwilling that he should see her expression as she waited for what was sure to come. 'Place your hand on a woman's heart. . . .' It was almost there when Gale twisted away, speaking lightly as she said,

'Isn't it a glorious evening? We're very lucky that it kept fine for the barbecue. I expect that in your country you have no such anxieties about the weather?'

He smiled, without humour, half turning from her.

'We certainly are able to plan events such as this without worry, yes.'

She raised her head, seeing him in profile, darkly in the sprinkled shafts of moonlight. The outline of his face was etched as if in stone; she noted the stern set jaw and aquiline nose, the low forehead, lined and aristocratic. The iron-grey colour of his hair certainly gave him an added distinction and she did wonder if he was aware of his incredible attractiveness.

'Tell me about your country?' she invited, still undecided whether or not to try out her charms on him.

He looked at her, then leant back against the trunk of the tree, resting his head against it.

'You've never been to Greece?' he asked and, as she shook her head, 'You should make an effort to visit it, Gale. Everyone should visit my country. Athens is a must, of course, but the islands—' He broke off and was silence for a space. 'The islands are something rather special. You would never regret having an island-hopping holiday.'

'I've heard of this. What exactly does one do?'

'Hop from one island to another.' He smiled at her, this time with a hint of amusement in his dark eyes. 'Not quite literally, as you know. The ferries are crossing all the time from one island to another. And the fares are ridiculously low; so are the hotels, so if you want to stay a few days you can. Then you get on a boat and go off to another island.'

'Are they all similar?'

'Not all, no.' Julius shook his head. 'You get the Aegean islands having a similarity, then you find that the Ionian islands also have a similarity, and so on.'

'Tell me about your island. Patmos, isn't it?'

'That's right. It's the most northerly of the Dodecanese Islands, and also the smallest. It's a volcanic island, of course, and many parts of it are barren. But it is a very beautiful island for all that, and the vegetation is in fact quite lush in parts.'

Gale listened as he went on, watching his changing expression and secretly owning that he was the most attractive male she had ever met. All others she could have forgotten ten minutes after having left them, but

Julius had lingered in her thoughts for a long while after they had said good-bye at the last party which they had both attended. There was a certain magnetic quality about him that seemed to draw even after he had departed. Gale recalled that she had been angry with herself in the end, and had made a determined effort to erase his image from her mind. She had succeeded . . . but here he was again, affecting her once more, although in what particular kind of way she could not have explained. He was talking now about the olive trees and the citrus fruits which flourished in the grounds of his house; he spoke of the view over the sea, and he spoke of other islands close by, which could easily be reached from Patmos.

'You must come,' he said again. 'Patmos is an island you'll never forget, once you have visited it.'

'It sounds wonderful.' Hitherto Gale had injected a cool note in her tone, but now it was absent and her voice had taken on a gentle quality unknown to Gale but certainly noticed by her companion, who looked fully into her face, taking in the lovely contours once more and seeming at the same time to be making a mental assessment. She thought of his bid to 'place a hand on her heart' and wondered how she would have fared had he not allowed her so easy a retreat.

'Yes, Gale, it is wonderful.' He spoke at last and she smiled up at him; he responded, saying, although rather absently, that it was time they were returning to the party.

'I expect we should be getting back,' Gale agreed . . . and yet, for some quite incomprehensible reason, she had the most strange desire to stay here with this handsome Greek, to stay and see what happened.

What did happen was something for which she was not in the least prepared, since she was expecting Julius to fall in step beside her as she moved away from the shade of the overhanging branches above her. Instead, he shot out a hand and caught her, pulling her up abruptly. In a flash she was in his arms, crushed against a body hard as steel, and his lips pressed hers in a kiss so ruthless and demanding that it might have come from Satan himself. There was no escape; Gale struggled vainly in his relentless grip, her body feeling bruised and her mouth crushed beneath his.

'I've wanted to do that from the first moment I saw you,' he said at last when, having satisfied himself, he drew away from her and gazed down into her hot face. 'I wonder if you know just how beautiful, and how tempting you are?'

Her eyes blazed; she lifted a clenched fist as if to strike him, but it was caught and held and Julius actually laughed as she fought to drag her hand away.

'You despicable – cad!' she cried, still pulling against his strong and easy hold upon her hand. 'How dared you? – and it wasn't as if I gave you the least atom of encouragement!'

'No?' with faint satire. 'You did, Gale— No, don't deny it, because that would be dishonest, and dishonesty in you would prove to be a disappointment to me. You were a trifle half-hearted, I admit, but that was merely owing to your indecision.' He stopped and then, coolly, his eyes intently fixed upon hers, 'You were endeavouring to decide whether or not to try out your wiles on me, as you have so often tried them out on others – with great success, so I have been informed.' His rich yet quiet voice, made more attractive by the trace of an accent, was edged with censure not untinged with humour. It would seem that while he disapproved of Gale's behaviour he at the same time had little sympathy for her victims. But this passed almost unnoticed by Gale, who literally gasped at his uncanny perception. It was incredible that he should make so accurate a reading of her mind. Mingling with her astonishment, however, was the equally strong emotion of anger; it mounted until it actually formed a hard blockage in her throat and for a while she found it impossible to articulate words. When at last she did speak, her voice quivered with fury.

'So you've been discussing me behind my back? I should like to know with whom!'

Julius smiled, that humourless smile she had seen on several previous occasions.

'It is not my intention to divulge the name of my informant,' he replied in cool dispassionate tones. 'As for our discussing you – a beautiful girl is always the object of discussion, you should be fully aware of that.' His grip on her hand slackened; she seized the opportunity of releasing it but, still aware of the pressure, she glanced down. A deep red mark portrayed the strength of the hand that had held hers and Gale's fury threatened to burst into an all-engulfing flame as she continued to stare at the mark which, even as she kept her gaze upon it, gradually took on a purple tinge. Julius stood looking down at her, his eyes glinting now, and before he spoke Gale had made a guess at his thoughts. 'You could have tried out your charms, Gale, but, with me, you'd have waited until hell freezes before you'd have made any headway.'

So soft the tone, yet vibrant with meaning. Gale went red, this time with discomfiture rather than anger. Here was a man to be avoided, she thought, recalling that, so short a time previously, her brother had firmly declared that Julius Spiridon would never go down in any battle, especially one involving a woman. Endeavouring to forget that kiss, and also her anger, she said, deciding on a dignified retreat from a formidable and impregnable adversary,

'We obviously understand one another, Julius. I'm sure you're wholly immune to the wiles of women – perhaps owing to considerable experience,' she could not resist adding with a sudden quizzical smile which served only to bring back the glint to his eye. 'Shall we return to the others? Our friends will be wondering where we are.'

For a long moment he made no move to comply with her suggestion, but stood there, gazing down into her face, an enigmatical expression on his.

'You're a strange girl,' he remarked at last, and his gaze now seemed to strip her naked. 'A very strange girl indeed – and a challenge. I'd like to see you again quite soon, but unfortunately I'm returning to Greece in a couple of days' time.'

Gale lifted her chin.

'It so happens, Julius, that I have no desire to see you again—'

'Don't lie,' he cut in calmly, suiting his pace to hers as she slowly began to walk away. 'I intrigue you just as much as you intrigue me. You'd dearly love to watch me succumb to your charms, just for the pleasure and satisfaction of throwing me over and letting me go off somewhere to lick my wounds, as so many others have been forced to do. I on the other hand would very much like to see *you* succumb to *my* – er – advances, shall we say? – as I'm not quite as confident of my charms as you are of yours.'

'How modest you are!' with undisguised sarcasm as Gale stopped and turned her head to look at him. 'I daresay, though, that you are well aware of your attractiveness as a man.' To her surprise he frowned heavily at this, just as if such outright flattery irritated him. He maintained a silence, the silence of admonition, and Gale was urged to terminate it before it caused her too much discomfort. 'So you would enjoy making me fall in love with you? – just for the pleasure of throwing me over?'

His dark eyes roved her again, unrestrained sensuality in their depths.

'Were I to make you fall in love with me,' he drawled, his tones adopting a rather lazy accent, 'there would be other pleasures to be enjoyed before I finally threw you over.'

Gale went hot, flashing him an almost murderous glance. Yet she was honest enough to admit to having asked for what she had received. Once again she resorted to icy reserve in an endeavour to extricate herself with dignity.

'Well, Julius,' she said, 'as neither of us will ever have the opportunity of deriving enjoyment from the other's downfall it seems we are to part friends. Shall we make it now, before either of us takes a step that might carry us over the border between friendship and enmity?'

His mouth curved; her blush deepened as she saw that he received her efforts at rhetoric with the utmost derision. He said, in that lazy drawl which was designed to supplement the impression of contempt he wished to convey,

'Our *au revoir* will come at the end of the evening, naturally, when the party breaks up. But we shall meet again – you know very well we shall – at another function such as this, just as we've met before.'

Gale frowned; she was not at all sure that she wanted another encounter with this dark and formidable Greek whose sparring finesse far surpassed her own. With men she liked to be in a position of superiority; if snubs were to be handed out she wished to be the one to do it. Such a position would never exist between Julius and herself – just the reverse, in fact, and this idea did not appeal to Gale in the least. Without commenting on his words she fell into step beside him as he began walking towards the lawn, on which several couples were dancing. The night was balmy and warm, the air sharp with the aroma of pines. Above, a full moon shed its light over the chalk downlands and the higher hills beyond. It was a night of unusual softness and Gale wondered if Julius had noticed its similarity to the atmosphere to which he was used, on his island in the Aegean. Strangely, the long silence existing between her and Julius held not a trace of awkwardness. On the contrary, it was almost companionable and Gale felt – much to her surprise – that had they not sparred in the way they had she could have derived an odd sort of pleasure from this quiet stroll. On reaching the lights proper she was claimed for a dance and she had no further words with Julius until they were saying goodnight on the illuminated forecourt where most of the cars had been parked.

'Goodnight, Gale . . . until we meet again.' Soft and subtle words, accompanied by a hint of amusement in his tone and a humorous lift of his straight dark brows. 'I shall be back in England next month.'

'We might not see one another,' she returned, unaware of the defensive quality of her voice. 'There aren't any parties in the offing that I know of.'

'Afraid?' he inquired, fixing her gaze. Her chin lifted. She said firmly,

'What have I to be afraid of? No man has ever put fear into me, Julius, and I'm very confident that none ever shall.'

'No man has ever put fear into you,' he repeated,

still holding her gaze. 'Unhappiness ... but not fear. And because one man caused you unhappiness every other man with whom you come into contact must suffer—' He broke off and laughed, shaking his head. 'No, that's not true, for not every man is stupid enough to fall victim to your wicked little schemes.' He remained amused – by his thoughts, she realized, wondering just what they were. She fell also to wondering who it was who had talked to Julius about her. It was faintly disconcerting to feel that her activities were known to others besides her brother and one or two of her friends. None of these would discuss her with Julius, she was absolutely certain of this. 'You'll learn in time, Gale – but you might find yourself getting hurt badly before the lesson finally gets through.'

'I'll not get hurt,' with confidence produced by past successes. 'I'm too hard-boiled for that.'

Humour lit his eyes, yet he was shaking his head in a sort of admonishing way.

'Bravado, my dear Gale,' he began, when she interrupted him.

'No such thing! I know what I'm about, Julius; make no mistake regarding that.'

He shrugged and said, carelessly now as if the subject were beginning to bore him a little,

'Watch *you* make no mistakes, Gale. Some women succeed brilliantly as adventuresses ... and some fail. They're not clever enough, nor are they cut out for that particular kind of life. Take heed of my warning before it's too late.'

CHAPTER TWO

JUST over a month later Gale received an invitation from Tricia's mother. Would she spend the week-end at Moorcroft House, as Tricia was ill and Mrs. Sims hoped that Gale's presence in the house would make her feel better.

Frowning, Gale stared for some time at the letter, then decided to telephone Mrs. Sims. What she heard made the blood freeze in Gale's veins. Tricia had been jilted and already there were rumours that Trevis was interested in the daughter of a titled man living in Cumberland. Gale knew that Trevis had a small fishing lodge up in Cumberland, and this was how he came to meet the girl, her father's estate being close to the place where the lodge was situated. Trevis's visits to the lodge, while Tricia was left behind, had always been a sore point with Gale, who had been Tricia's friend for several years. Gale had secretly thought that Trevis should have spent all his leisure time with his fiancée, but instead he liked to go to the lodge where, he said, he could rest from the rigours of business life. At first he had gone up there about once a month, but recently he had been spending almost every week-end at the lodge and although Tricia was naturally upset about this she was also very sweet and understanding about it, telling the indignant Gale that Trevis really did need the rest. Rest! thought Gale now as she stood by the phone, having replaced the receiver after promising to go over to the Sims' home first thing the following morning and staying until Sunday night. Men! Rotters, all of them! How Gale wished she could work some miracle that would result in Trevis receiving the punishment he so thoroughly deserved. The thought of this remained with Gale as she drove her car along the lovely lane leading to the small village of Denehurst in Kent where the Sims' eighteenth-century house was situated.

Tricia was upstairs in her bedroom when Gale arrived. She spent all her time there, Mrs. Sims told Gale, actually weeping as she talked. Gale swallowed something hard and painful in her throat, thinking of the lovely wedding dress already partly made, and the bridesmaids' dresses too. Gale was to have been the chief bridesmaid and already she had had several fittings. History repeating itself – and no one could know better than Gale just what her friend was suffering. This was probably the chief reason for Mrs. Sims sending for her, since she knew that the same thing had once happened to Gale.

'We can't do anything with her,' wept Mrs. Sims, her face pale and drawn. 'She's going to be ill – have a breakdown or something if she continues like this. All she does is lie on her bed and cry. It's dreadful to see how she suffers!'

Fury surged within Gale. She felt she would have murdered Trevis had he been present. How could he be so utterly heartless? And Tricia so gentle and so very lovely, with her soft brown eyes and elfin-like features. She had been so trusting, too, never for one moment suspecting her fiancé of doing anything more than resting, and of course fishing, a pastime which he liked immensely, he had once told Gale. Fishing! thought Gale now, her mouth curving into a cynical line that was far from pretty to see. Fishing! Well, that was what he had been doing – in his own particular way.

'You said on the phone that already there were

rumours about Trevis and this girl. How have they got round so soon?'

'Perhaps you don't know, but Trevis lets his friends have the lodge when he's not using it himself. It seems that one of them was up there with his wife and it was she who heard the gossip in the village post office. The story soon spread once this couple got home and naturally it reached Tricia's ears. She tackled Trevis and – and—' Mrs. Sims broke off, overcome by her tears. 'Trevis admitted it,' she added at length. 'And he told Tricia that he was breaking the engagement, as he wanted to marry this other girl. I'm sure it's mainly because of her father's position – his title, I mean, since Trevis himself will be a very wealthy man some day, when anything happens to his uncle.'

'He's actually got as far as wanting to marry this girl?' Gale's voice was sharp with disgust and her lovely mouth was drawn into a thin and almost ugly line. 'He must have been carrying on with her for some time, that's pretty obvious.' She was thinking of Malcolm, who had been two-timing her for a long while before someone took it upon herself to put Gale in possession of the fact.

'Yes, he must have been seeing her regularly, every time he went up there. It's easily explained now why he began going so often – and there was my poor Tricia, defending him, saying he required complete rest because he was overworked.'

Gale was silent a while and then, rising from her chair,

'I'll go up to her. She doesn't know about my coming, you said?'

'No, I felt she might not like the idea, so I didn't tell her. Go up, Gale dear, and see if you can do anything to comfort her.' Mrs. Sims shook her head miserably.

'Time is the only thing – as it was with you.'

Gale nodded, too full to speak. It hurt abominably to see her friend's mother like this. But it hurt even more when she saw her friend, lying face downwards on the bed, her shoulders heaving as the silent sobs racked her small slim body. Standing by the door, Gale could not stem her own tears and as Tricia had not become aware of her presence she went along to the bathroom and splashed cold water over her eyes, drying them on a towel. It would not do Tricia much good to see Gale crying, or even to notice evidence of tears, and so Gale waited a few moments until, a glance in the mirror telling her all traces of her own emotion were erased, she returned to the bedroom and, bending over the weeping girl, put a gentle arm around her, speaking soothingly to her as she did so. Startled, Tricia turned on her side, blinking at Gale through her tears. Her face was blotched and swollen, her eyes glazed by misery.

'Your mother asked me to come for the week-end,' Gale explained at once. 'Why didn't you yourself contact me, Tricia, and tell me what had happened?'

'I couldn't tell anyone—' Tricia stopped as a great sob rose from the very heart of her. 'You s-see, I th-thought he would c-come back to me.'

'We all do, when anything like this happens.' Gale's voice was grim despite its soothing edge. 'You don't realize it now, Tricia dear, but he isn't worth a thought.'

'That's what Mother and Father say, but if he were to come back to me I'd forgive him.'

Gale was silent; she herself had felt like that for weeks after Malcolm had let her down. It was only with the passing of time that she had come to admit that he was not worth having. It would be the same with Tricia, but unfortunately there was much suffering to be endured before the stage of forgetfulness was reached.

'Come,' Gale encouraged, 'get up and we'll go into town. I've a present to get for my mother's birthday and you can help me choose it.'

Tricia was shaking her head even while Gale spoke.

'You're kind, Gale, and Mother meant well when she sent for you, but I don't want company. I just want to stay here by myself.' Her voice broke and tears flowed once more. Gale said gently,

'Remember that I know exactly how you're feeling. I also know that I myself would have been far better off had I listened to the well-meaning people who tried to help me, but like you I wanted only to be alone. Eventually I did snap out of it and accept help, and you'll see, Tricia dear, that I'm right when I say you'll feel a little better if you talk, and if you come downstairs instead of remaining up here. Have you had anything to eat today?' And when Tricia shook her head, 'Then we'll call at that nice Swiss restaurant and have lunch. We went there the last time I was here, remember?'

Tricia nodded, and to Gale's satisfaction she sat up, wiping her eyes with a sodden handkerchief. Handing her a clean one Gale continued to talk in her soft persuasive tones and at last Tricia agreed to accompany Gale into town. That the agreement was made merely for politeness, owing to Gale's continued perseverance, mattered not in the least; it was sufficient that Tricia was stirred to move at all, for if she insisted in her stubbornness then a breakdown would be inevitable.

Mrs. Sims stared disbelievingly when the two girls

appeared; her eyes met those of Gale in a silent message of thanks.

'We're going into town,' Gale explained, going on to say that as it was her mother's birthday the following Tuesday she wanted to buy her present. 'Don't expect us back for lunch, Mrs. Sims; we're having it out.'

'That's fine.' A smile touched Mrs. Sims' lips as she looked affectionately at her daughter. 'Buy yourself something nice, dear. I'll give you some money—'

'No, Mother – thank you all the same.' Tricia's lips trembled as she added, 'What's the use buying anything now?'

'I didn't mean clothes, dear. Buy yourself a new bag or a pretty piece of jewellery.'

'Jewellery? Who would I wear it for?'

Mrs. Sims flushed and Gale instantly filled the breach, saying they had better be on their way, otherwise they would be too late to get a lunch.

Tricia ate nothing anyway, even though Gale made several persuasive attempts to induce her to try the delicious food put before them.

'I can't!' Tricia's eyes filled up. 'Gale, I know it's awful of me, but I don't want to live.' She stared at Gale across the table, lost and desperately unhappy. Fury surged through Gale's veins. If only there were a way of making Trevis suffer! Gale felt she would go to extreme lengths, should a way present itself to her.

But it was Tricia herself who came out with an idea – on the Sunday evening just before Gale was leaving, after promising to come again the following weekend.

'All my love seems to have turned to hate,' she said unexpectedly, avoiding Gale's eyes as she looked down at her hands, clasped tightly in her lap. The two girls were in Gale's room, Gale having just finished packing her suitcase ready for the maid to carry down to her car. 'I'd like nothing better than to frame him.'

'Frame?' Gale looked interrogatingly at her friend, who nodded but still avoided her gaze.

'Yes, frame – and so prevent his marrying that girl.'

'I know just how you feel, because I felt the same; but it's impossible. There's absolutely nothing you can do, Tricia.'

A long pause and then, rather timidly,

'There is something that can be done . . . but you wouldn't agree.'

'Me? Am I involved?' Gale looked into her face as Tricia at last raised her head. The tragic expression still invaded her eyes, but deep and almost venomous hatred lingered there too. Tricia's voice was tight and hard as she answered,

'He could be framed, Gale – framed in a way that would in fact be fairly simple.' She paused again and then blurted out what was in her mind. Stunned that the gentle Tricia should even have thought up such an idea, let alone voice it, Gale could only stare in speechless amazement, while Tricia blushed and began fidgeting with her hands.

'It wouldn't work. . . .' Emphasized words, yet Gale's voice faded as she spoke, her brain working furiously despite her efforts to thrust the preposterous idea from her. Why not? she asked herself, but no sooner had she done so than she became so scared that her heartbeats actually increased to a sickening speed. Trevis might become violent – or, even worse, he might do her the sort of injury which any self-respecting girl wished to avoid at all costs.

'What sort of a man is Trevis?' Gale found herself asking, and was told to her surprise that he was quiet, and that he had no temper at all. 'Are you sure?' persisted Gale, her heartbeats still causing her some discomfiture. She could not do this thing, much as she would like to, for undoubtedly Trevis deserved to receive the same treatment he had extended to Tricia – which was to be jilted by this girl whom he soon hoped to marry.

'Quite sure, Gale. I've never seen him in a temper – nor even impatient with me. He – he was always so gentle. . . .' She tailed off as a sob caught her throat. Yet despite her emotion she still retained that expression of hatred as she went on to elaborate on the idea she had thought up. 'Trevis will be at the lodge next week-end, but Louise won't be at home—'

'How do you know this?' interrupted Gale sharply, and added, before her friend could reply, 'You haven't mentioned her name before. I took it for granted that you didn't know it.'

'Trevis told me her name,' whispered Tricia in husky tones. 'He also told me that she was going to her grandmother's next week-end.'

Gale frowned heavily.

'He actually talked about this girl to you?'

'Only at the end, of course, when he was – was breaking the engagement. I – I asked him about her and he told me her name, and that she visited her grandmother once a month – spent the first week-end of every month with her.' Tricia paused, waiting for some comment, but Gale was too disgusted to speak. That Trevis could actually tell his fiancée about this other girl! What an utter cad he must be! 'As I was saying, Trevis will be at the lodge, but he won't be seeing Louise. If you went there and – and did as I suggested, I could telephone her father very early in the morning telling him that the man who aspired to marry his daughter was at the lodge with one of his girl-friends, and that if he went there he would find proof of this.'

Gale stared again, speechlessly. Tricia was so calm now, although her face was pallid and drawn. She sat there, looking at Gale through wide beseeching eyes; it was plain that her mind was now totally absorbed with the idea of revenge, just as Gale's had been when Malcolm had acted in a similar way to Trevis. It struck Gale that Tricia might from now on follow the path taken by Gale herself and a frown creased her high forehead. Such a path would not do for the gentle Tricia; she was too vulnerable, while Gale herself had acquired an armour of defence against all men. She was fully convinced that her own once gentle heart was now made of stone.

'It can't be done, Tricia.' Gale shook her head emphatically . . . and yet she found herself becoming more and more immersed in the idea. 'I couldn't possibly get away with it.'

'I've been to the lodge, once,' said Tricia, appearing not to have heard what Gale had said. 'There are two bedrooms, but Trevis told me he never even enters the small one, which is right at the end of the passage which runs the whole length of the lodge. Trevis – and any of his friends who might happen to go there in his absence – always uses the big room, which is close to the lounge, and has its own bathroom. Trevis said that he might as well not have the small room for what use it is to him.' Tricia glanced at Gale, but saw only a masked countenance from which it was impossible to gather anything. 'You could get the key from the outhouse, where it's always kept, on a shelf. Then, after letting yourself in, you could open a window – there is only one floor, incidentally, so the bedrooms are on ground level. You could then lock the door from the outside, replace the key, and re-enter through the window, and hide yourself in the small bedroom – or you could even go to bed, for Trevis would not find you. As I've mentioned, he never arrives at the lodge until the early hours of Saturday morning and, as he says himself, he wants only to fall into bed and sleep until late the following day.' Tricia stopped at last, her eyes on her friend's face. Gale was deep in thought, common sense battling with the growing urge to fall in with Tricia's plan and give Trevis the lesson he deserved.

'It's altogether too risky,' she frowned, shaking her head. 'Supposing Trevis just did decide to look into that room?'

'He wouldn't, certainly not at that time, when he'd driven all that way. Besides, there's no reason why he should look in; there's only a small camp bed in there – nothing else at all.'

Faintly Gale smiled. She remarked rather dryly,

'So it would, were I to fall in with your suggestion, be a long dreary time of cold comfort for me?'

'You needn't go into the room until midnight at the earliest, and if I phone Louise's father about seven on the Saturday morning he'd be there by half past – or perhaps a little later.' Tricia shrugged. 'You'd then be free to leave.'

'Free to leave?' Gale's brows shot up. How could anyone be so naïve? 'What is Trevis made of? I'd be in my night clothes, remember. He might just decide to pay me back for ruining his chances with this Louise. I certainly can't see him letting me off scot free.'

'You mean he might force you to—?' Tricia's eyes opened wide. 'Never; he isn't like that at all!'

'My dear Tricia,' said Gale with a return to her previous dry tone, 'all men are like that.'

'But you could take care of yourself in any case,' responded Tricia with confidence, and Gale could not help but laugh.

'I expect I'd put up a good show in an emergency,' she admitted, but went on to point out that a girl as scantily dressed as she would be was at a disadvantage to begin with.

'Trevis wouldn't try anything on, Gale, truly he wouldn't. Besides, he'd be too upset even to *think*.'

Gale said nothing for the moment. The idea appealed to her immensely even though her more prudent tract of mind warned her of the hazards. There was much more to it than the mere hiding herself in the spare room and making her entrance when she heard Louise's father arrive. This particular situation she felt she could deal with successfully, since Trevis would be so utterly confounded that he would in all probability be unable to collect his wits before his visitor made his swift and wrathful departure. It was what would happen afterwards that troubled Gale, for she could hardly see Trevis being in anything other than a burning rage. Yet would he dare to do her an injury? Tricia maintained that he would not even be able to think, and on giving the matter a little more thought Gale found herself inclined to agree about this.

'Are – are you considering my suggestion?' queried Tricia with a hopeful glance.

'Trevis certainly ought to be paid out for what he's done to you,' replied Gale pensively, staring rather vacantly at the wall in front of her. 'It's a simple plan, as you said, and even though Trevis will undoubtedly guess that you were at the bottom of it there isn't much he can do, because he doesn't know me – neither by sight nor by name. So there couldn't be any reprisals – not once I'd made my initial escape, that is.'

'You *are* going to do it!' exclaimed Tricia. 'Thank you, Gale.'

A faint smile played about Gale's mouth. Clearly Tricia, blinded by the thought of revenge on her unfaithful lover, seemed not to anticipate the slightest difficulty in the carrying out of the plan she had devised. This was probably owing to the fact that Gale herself was always so efficient in all she did, possessing more than her share of confidence. Added to this was the established dislike of men in general which Gale was not averse to revealing to Tricia; this latter would naturally make Tricia more confident of her co-operation. Gale's smile deepened as this last word crossed her mind; Tricia was to do very little – just get up early and telephone Louise's father. Not that it mattered; Gale was capable of carrying out the major part of the operation. Nevertheless, much as the idea appealed she cautiously told Tricia that she must give it a little more consideration, and despite Tricia's disappointment at not receiving an immediate assurance it was left that way. But, driving home later, and after dwelling on the idea for some time, Gale knew she would not be able to resist putting it into operation.

She drove her car along the motorway, heading north. For some years she had promised herself a visit to the Lake District, having heard over and over again just how beautiful it was, but never had she visualized herself going up there for any reason other than a holiday. This was a daring escapade, but it was becoming all the while more and more attractive because of it. And, should it go off without a hitch, there would be an end-product of immense satisfaction in the knowledge that Trevis had got his deserts.

The journey was long and tedious, but at last Gale

arrived at Ennerdale where she booked in at an hotel for the night. The following morning she drove through several high passes in the mountain range, absorbing the magnificent scenery despite the fact of her mind's being almost fully occupied with what was to come. Arriving at Swathemore Beck she saw on her right the mansion of Louise's father, standing on a rise and surrounded by gardens and wooded knolls. Gale drove on; having drawn a map from Tricia's description of the area, she knew exactly where the lodge was situated, just about a mile from the big house. The road ran along the beck, then curved towards the squat stone building almost hidden by trees and other wild vegetation. The sight of it seemed to give the plan a stark reality it had not possessed before and in spite of her calm manner and steadfast resolution Gale was acutely conscious of tensed nerves, and a fluttering sensation in the region of her stomach. This was the first occasion in which real danger had entered into her activities, and although she was impatient of her apprehension she had in fairness to herself to admit it was only natural that she should feel like this. It would be worth it in the end, though, she told herself again; Trevis would be punished and Tricia would at least have the satisfaction of knowing he had lost the girl for whom he had so callously thrown her over.

As there was still plenty of time to spare Gale had an opportunity to look around. Having found the key on the shelf in the outhouse where Tricia had said it would be, Gale entered the lodge. It seemed a little cold and when she entered the small room where she was to conceal herself a distinct smell of must assailed her nostrils and she grimaced. Cold comfort indeed, she thought, her eyes straying to the camp bed on which she would later be trying to rest. Emerging from the tiny apartment, she walked the length of the corridor before entering the lounge, a comfortable room but not particularly tidy, there being all sorts of fishing tackle lying about. She went into the bedroom; this was also comfortable, with the bed neatly made and the curtains partly drawn across the low, wide window. Gale's eyes were drawn to the dressing-table. On it, framed in gilt, was a photograph of a pretty girl of about nineteen years of age. Disgusted, Gale left the room.

Apart from the kitchen and a small bathroom leading off the main bedroom there was nothing more to the lodge – except the wild mass of unkempt vegetation which practically surrounded it and which could be described as its 'spacious grounds'.

The next thing was to take her suitcase from the car and then drive right into the vegetation, so that the vehicle was completely hidden from view.

A deep silence reigned over everything; here was peace and wild beauty, many of the scenic features being the result of glaciation, and of course, the superimposed drainage pattern inherited from a bygone geological era when a deep sedimentary cover lay over the ancient contorted rocks now revealed. Gale stood a long while, gazing around in appreciation of the scenery, then picked up her suitcase from the step where she had put it on taking it from the car. Placing it out of sight in a small fitted cupboard in the room she was to occupy, Gale went along to the kitchen and, filling and switching on the electric kettle she calmly made herself a cup of tea, which she drank while eating the sandwiches made up for her by the proprietor of the hotel.

So cool and collected she was now; it was as if she had entered into a state of mental inertia where nothing could touch her, let alone leave the way open for any emotional stress. It was unnatural – uncanny, almost, she thought, sitting there on a high stool in the area of the kitchen which she supposed could be described as the dinette. She glanced through the window, again absorbing the delightful spectacle of changing colour as the less hardy trees gave way to the pines and other alpine vegetation. This was certainly a lovely spot in which to own a retreat, and Gale could not help thinking how Tricia would have enjoyed coming here when she and Trevis were married. Anger rose within her and she set her mouth, more determined than ever to make Trevis pay for his crime.

Having finished her sandwiches she washed the crockery and put it away, making sure to leave everything exactly as she found it. Then she went into the lounge and sat down, determined not to go into that cold musty room until much later, for it was not necessary to spend the whole evening in there when Trevis was not expected until after midnight.

But it was less than an hour later when she heard the car crunch to a standstill on the path outside, and her flesh began to creep. Not already! It was only half past eight; Trevis must have left much earlier than usual. Like lightning Gale reached the door and shot through it, running silently along the corridor to the small bedroom, where she stood by the closed window and tried to look through the chink in the curtains, but she could see nothing. She heard a light step, then the door of the outhouse creaking, as it had when she herself opened it. She had put the key back on the shelf and mentally she followed Trevis's movements as he reached for it.

Then Gale heard the front door opening and closing, and the light tread as Trevis covered the small area of corridor leading into the sitting-room. She held her breath, trying to convince herself that he would not enter the small bedroom, even though he had arrived early and would not be ready to fall into bed, as Tricia had so confidently asserted he would. The lounge door closed and silence pervaded the house. He must be reading, she surmised, still standing by the window, mentally calculating how many dreary hours she must remain here before she was safely in her car and travelling south again.

The silence continued and Gale sat down on the camp bed; it was almost two hours since Trevis's arrival and he hadn't moved from the lounge. But a few minutes later she heard him go into the kitchen, and later still he returned to the lounge – with a supper tray, she surmised, suddenly realizing she would have given anything for a cup of tea.

It was well after twelve when at last she heard him enter his bedroom, closing the door after him. And only then did she breathe freely. The worst was over, she thought, managing to lie down and hoping she would be able to snatch a few hours' sleep. This she did, though it was a fitful rest and she woke at intervals until at six-thirty she got up and tidied her hair. She had sachets with her, soaked in eau de Cologne, and these she used on her face and hands, being unable to wash. Tricia was to phone Louise's father at seven o'clock, so he should be here fairly soon after that, as it was unlikely he would lose much time in discovering for himself whether or not the call was genuine. Gale fell to visualizing this unknown man receiving the message; he'd be in bed most likely, and probably his temper would be frayed at the outset, having his rest disturbed at so early an hour.

Gale became tensed as the moments slipped away, and her nerves were fluttering in spite of her most determined effort at control. She was ready, dressed in a frilly nightdress which was slightly longer than the transparent negligé she wore. Damning evidence, she thought, glancing down. The finale should be over and done with in a matter of seconds. . . .

She heard the car stop, then the slamming of the door followed by a sharp rap on the front door of the lodge. A few moments' silence, then voices. The loud imperious tones of the caller reached Gale, though not too clearly; Trevis's voice was merely a low indistinct murmur.

'Who the devil . . .?' Another few words Gale could not make out and then, 'I've just received a phone call and was given to understand it was. . . .' Gale missed the rest, but in any case now was the time to make her dramatic entrance, yet she hesitated, her heart naturally beating over-rate. Taking a deep breath, she at last emerged and trod silently along the corridor towards the lounge, into which Trevis had taken his visitor.

'Trevis darling, what's wrong? I heard voices—' She stopped, gaping at one of the occupants of the room in stunned disbelief, while every drop of blood drained from her cheeks. 'Julius,' she managed to stammer at last, 'wh-what are y-you d-doing here?' She was oblivious of the obese man standing there, staring at her with a sort of furious incomprehension. 'I – you. . . .' Automatically she drew together the edges of her negligé as, after an involuntary start and a glance of disbelief, the tall Greek allowed his eyes to sweep an all-embracing glance from her face to her toes, peeping through her dainty strapped slippers, and then back over every line and curve of her body again.

'Isn't it I who should be asking what you are doing here?' responded Julius pleasantly, and all Gale could find to say was,

'I thought it would be Trevis whom I should meet.'

'Can one of you tell me what's going on?' interposed Louise's father, blustering, and exceedingly red in the face.

'Undoubtedly you thought it would be Trevis,' commented Julius, ignoring the interruption and idly tying the cord of his dressing-gown as it slid undone, having been hurriedly fastened in the first place. 'Obviously you didn't come here with the intention of sleeping with him, so I can't think for the moment why you should be here at all.' He stopped, one side of his mouth curving upwards as Gale coloured swiftly at his words. 'This man here had begun to say something about a phone call from some unknown woman who informed him that—' Julius broke off, frowning. 'You'd better begin again,' he told the man. 'I hadn't even got the gist of it before we were interrupted by my friend here.'

'*Your* friend?' snapped the man, glaring at Julius. 'I was given to understand that she was Trevis's friend, and that he was staying here with her. *Is* Trevis here?' he demanded suddenly, his eyes suspicious all at once.

'I came alone,' replied Julius quietly. 'Trevis didn't wish to come because his girl-friend was away – so I was informed by the friend who arranged for me to come up here for the week-end. I personally don't know this Trevis, but I seemed to gather that he spends most of his week-ends here with her, at the fishing lodge—'

'At the lodge!' The man's face took on a distinctly purple tinge. 'Young man, you're speaking about my daughter! Trevis sees her, but at the Hall – my home,' he elucidated, then added, 'Are you quite sure he isn't here now?'

'That's what I've just said,' returned Julius, stifling a yawn in a bored, impatient sort of way. 'Gale, you had better do the explaining.' He swept an imperious hand towards a chair. 'Sit down.' It was an order, quietly but emphatically given, and Gale's chin lifted. But instantly she knew the reason for the order. Too much was revealed because her negligé had come open again. She obeyed, more colour fusing her cheeks as, catching the old man's gaze, she realized he had actually been enjoying the free show of feminine curves. Decidedly put out, at least for the moment, Gale lowered her lashes. Julius repeated his request for an explanation but, unwilling to do this before Louise's father, she glanced up, a message in her eyes which she sincerely hoped he would receive. He stared down into her face for a long moment before saying,

'On second thoughts, Gale, we'll talk in private.' He turned to the waiting, expectant man at his side. 'I can only offer my apologies for any inconvenience you have been caused, and ask you to leave.'

'Leave!' he exploded. 'I demand to know why I've been brought out here. I was told I'd find my future son-in-law with another girl, and instead I find a foreigner with his – his—' The words came to an abrupt halt as Julius's expression changed.

'Yes,' he murmured silkily, 'you were about to say?'

But the man must have decided that prudence was the best policy, for he merely blustered for a while, declaring he would get in touch with Trevis immediately and demand an explanation from him.

'It's clear that you were expecting him to be here,' he snapped at Gale, 'because you've already said so!'

Julius was at the door, holding it open; the man glared as he passed him and a moment later his car could be heard roaring down the weed-strewn path running from the house to the gate.

'And now,' invited Julius softly as he turned to Gale, 'perhaps you will enlighten me?'

CHAPTER THREE

A DEEP silence settled on the room when Gale finished speaking; it was the silence of disbelief on Julius's part and the silence of embarrassment on Gale's. It was far from pleasant to be forced to relate a story such as she had just told to Julius, not only because she must confess to an action which she knew full well would be considered perfidious in the extreme, but also because it was a story of failure. Trevis would now escape punishment, and this irked Gale simply owing to her confidence in the success of the plan, a plan doomed to failure at the outset because of Tricia's mistaken assumption that Trevis had meant to come up here this week-end. Instead, he must have let it be known among his friends that the lodge was free for anyone wanting it. Gale had gathered from what Julius said that a mutual friend of his and Trevis had arranged that Julius could have the lodge – either for the fishing or merely for a rest and change of scenery; the reason was of no importance whatsoever. What was important was that he was here at all, so being the cause of the humiliation through which Gale was now passing. His searching eyes were on her face, censorious and yet faintly disbelieving in spite of the full confession she had just made.

'To say I'm amazed at your action is putting it mildly indeed,' he observed at last. 'I said you were a strange girl; I did not expect to discover that you were also possessed of criminal tendencies.'

'I'm not aware of having asked for your opinion of me,' she returned icily, getting to her feet. 'As there's

nothing more we have to say to one another perhaps you'll excuse me. I must get started for home.'

His dark eyes flickered unrestrainedly over her; she experienced a sudden quiver of nerves and caught the edges of her negligé together with rather more haste than delicacy, and her companion's lips curved in amusement.

'You came by car, I take it?'

She nodded.

'It's outside.'

'Effectively tucked away out of sight, eh?' He moved, coming forward into the middle of the room. Instinctively she stepped back and his smile of amusement deepened. 'I said we'd meet again, remember?' His tones were soft, like the purring of a satisfied cat, she thought, trying not to let her imagination run away with her. 'I never expected us to meet like this, though.' Julius paused as his lips quivered with mirth. 'What an opportunity!'

Nerves quivered again; he was only joking, of course . . . and yet Gale sent a glance over her shoulder. The door was closed. Swallowing something hard in her throat, she said, striving to keep her voice steady,

'No doubt you consider this situation amusing—'

'Vastly amusing,' he cut in pleasantly.

'But your amusement is to be short-lived; I'm leaving in a few minutes, when I've got dressed.'

'You are?' with an odd and unfathomable inflection.

'Of course. There isn't anything for me to stay for now. You – you don't want me disturbing you.' She looked into his eyes, riveted upon her, a glimmer of amusement in their depths . . . but there was something else there, something that caused her heartbeats to race, and led her automatically to size him up, as if she

would measure her chances against him in physical combat. She could have derived some amusement from that, had she not been fully concerned with her precarious position. 'Place your hand on a woman's heart and she's yours instantly. . . .' The words, spoken with such derision, came back to Gale once more as she continued to meet his gaze, afraid of what she saw . . . and yet fascinated by it.

'You wouldn't be disturbing me,' laughed Julius at length. 'On the contrary, you'd be entertaining me.'

'Don't be ridiculous! What sort of a woman do you think I am?'

His dark eyes flickered; he seemed to fall into a moment of deep thought.

'Are you trying to tell me you're a . . . good woman?'

She coloured, forgetting the danger for a space as anger rose.

'You might not think so, but I am!'

He cocked an eyebrow.

'Come, Gale, don't try to convince me you've a hundred-per-cent escape record – not the way you play about with the men, leading them on and then throwing them over.'

'Certainly I have!'

'Then all I can say is they're not men at all. You'd have paid dear if you'd tried any of your tricks on me.' He paused, expecting her to comment, but she kept silent. 'Perhaps you've never played such a dangerous game as this before?' And when she shook her head in a sort of mechanical gesture, 'Did you expect to emerge from an escapade such as this entirely unscathed?' He teetered forward; the action startled her owing to its swiftness and unexpectedness and she took another step backwards, an action which brought to his eyes a

return of that glimmer of amusement.

'I didn't expect any retaliation from Trevis, if that is what you mean?' Which was not entirely true, for Gale had experienced certain misgivings even though Tricia had assured her that Trevis 'wasn't like that at all'.

A sceptical lift of Julius's brows and then,

'I can't believe it. Such naïveté is totally out of character. You must have recognized the risk, and accepted it.'

'I expect I could have held my own,' he returned with a slight toss of her head.

'Just depends on how big this Trevis is. Do you suppose you could hold your own with me?' Subtle tones and that expression in his eyes again. Gale licked her lips. This man wasn't safe to be with; he was far far too confident, in that particular kind of way that seemed to stamp him a rake, a seducer – as her brother had described him that night at the barbecue.

'I don't know that your question is relevant,' she returned shortly. 'In fact, it's rather ridiculous....' Her voice faltered away to silence as without warning Julius covered the distance between them in three languid strides. Her pulse beginning to race, she slid a hand behind her, feeling for the door handle. 'I'm g-going to get dr'dressed now,' she managed to add in spite of her fluttering nerves and quickened heartbeats. The man was dangerous; she distrusted the sensuous pursing of his lips and the darkening of his eyes, as if something smouldered there, ready to burst into flame. Yet despite the acknowledgment of danger Gale was acutely aware of some exciting depth of emotion which the formidable Greek awakened in her, not for the first time. Without doubt he possessed a dynamic personality which if exerted to the full would be a severe test to any woman, however virtuous basically. 'Time's getting on—' Gale inserted a light note into her voice as she felt the door handle between her fingers. 'It's always better to begin a long journey early in the morning – when you're fresh.'

He smiled, a rather crooked smile, and satirical.

'What you say is doubtless true, my dear . . . but it's far too early to set out for all that. In fact,' he added in the tone she had already likened to the purr of a satisfied cat, 'it's much too early to be up at all.' And without affording her the opportunity of dodging out of his way he had her in his arms, crushing her to him, his mouth pressed to hers. She struggled, just as on that other occasion, but she was helpless against strength such as his. Without effort he held her, forcing his kisses on her, one hand moving subtly, almost imperceptibly towards the place beneath which her heart was racing abnormally. 'Don't fight, Gale,' he whispered in a voice low and hoarse. 'Come, let us enjoy ourselves—'

'Leave me alone! I'll have you jailed if you so much as touch me!'

'You expect me to allow you to go? My dear Gale, a man would have to be made of stone not to exploit a situation such as this. And I'm no stone. I assure you; on the contrary, I'm a Greek . . . and surely you know our reputation?' Smooth and faintly tinged with humour were his tones all at once. Gale renewed her struggles, afraid of a man for the first time in her life.

But also for the first time in her life she was afraid of herself.

'Take your hands off me!' she cried, at last abandoning a struggle which she had known at the outset would be futile. 'I've told you, I'm going home!' But even before the last word was out Julius had opened the door and, with as much ease as if he were handling a doll, he swung Gale off her feet and carried her into the room which he had occupied during the night. 'You'll be sorry for this,' she cried, her throat becoming dry and blocked as she watched him close the door and begin untying the girdle of his dressing-gown. 'You haven't given a moment's thought to the consequences—'

'My dear girl,' he interrupted with humour, 'this is hardly the situation where one spends precious time considering consequences. Let's dwell only on the pleasures to come, and on the romance of this position in which we find ourselves.' He was slipping off his dressing-gown his body close to the door, in case she should make an effort to escape, she realized, pressing a hand against her heart because its thudding actually frightened her. Could she possibly escape from a situation such as this? With sinking hopes she began to plead, feeling this might prove more effective than an attitude of angry protest and aggression. But Julius merely smiled as he listened, then said casually that it was time she knew what fear was. She might now think twice before taking it upon herself to make some poor man suffer. There was not an atom of pity in the whole of his make-up, Gale decided, noting the firm, clear-cut outline of his features and the prominent chin and high cheekbones which were always present in the classical representation of the pagan Greek gods whose images were so numerously carved in stone. Pagan he appeared at this moment, pagan and ruthlessly determined to have his way . . . and to satisfy his desire.

'You're going to regret this,' she quivered, her eyes filling up as he came towards her. 'I – shan't l-let you get away with it.'

He stopped a second, looking at her across the intervening space as she stood with her back to the bed, not having moved since he put her down.

'There'll be no regrets on my part, Gale.' He moved again, and reached her. This time his arms were gentle and his voice soft as he continued, 'And I have a feeling there won't be any on your part either. In fact, I'm optimistic enough to believe that we might both decide to continue our little affair indefinitely—'

'*I* shall not!' she flashed, her cheeks cold and white. 'The only thing I'll feel for you is hatred!'

Again he smiled, shaking his head.

'Isn't it a little early to make a statement like that? Wait until it's all over; your reactions might surprise you.'

She stared, speechless for an incredulous moment as, held firmly but gently by the arms, she looked up into his face.

'Modesty certainly isn't one of your virtues,' she told him with a sneer of contempt.

'Nor is insincerity one of my vices,' he returned imperturbably. 'I've had enough experience of women's reactions to know whether or not they enjoy my lovemaking.'

Gale was silent a while, thinking of this and allowing her imagination full rein. That he would be the perfect lover she had no doubt, so what he implied was probably true. Women would derive exceeding pleasure from his advances.

'Have you had lots of women?' She hadn't really meant to ask that, and she wondered if she had been impelled to do by the natural instinct of playing for time.

'I expect it could be termed lots.' The casual way in which he answered her spoke volumes. Not one of these women had made the slightest impression on him. He had taken and enjoyed them, then cast them off without so much as a second thought to what their particular feelings might be. Gale wondered just how many of these unfortunates had fallen in love with the handsome and inordinately attractive Greek. For undoubtedly it would not be difficult to fall in love with him, unless of course one was on one's guard – as Gale now was, since she had already owned to herself that he affected her as no other man ever had before. He moved restlessly and her spirits sank right into her feet as she was drawn close to him in a hard and possessive embrace. Her lips were claimed in a long and ardent kiss; her body was pressed close to his so that she could feel his heart throbbing against her. 'You're so beautiful,' he whispered with vibrant emotion. 'Give in willingly, Gale, so that you can find as much pleasure as I.' His arm tightened, crushing her even closer, and his hand sought and found the place over her heart.

'Don't,' she implored, finding herself carried away on the tide of his passion. 'Let me go . . . *please*!'

'You don't really want me to let you go. Be honest and admit it.' His accents were lowered to a throaty bass tone, which vibrated with suppressed passion; his lips caressed her cheek with a sort of tantalizing persuasion that was an art in itself, forcing a warm glow to spread through her whole body. 'Stop fighting and come to me—'

'Never!' she cut in with the desperation of a last defensive stand. 'Never – not willingly, that is!' She managed to pull herself away, hitting out at his chest with her small clenched fists. Not in her wildest imagination could she have seen herself in so precarious a position as this. Nothing could save her. Resignedly she admitted this even while she alternately threatened and pleaded, tears blurring her vision. 'I scarcely know you – it's ridiculous that you could even suggest that I –

that we—' Her words were smothered by his lips; she came close unresistingly as his arms tightened like hawsers round her small slender body. What was the use of exhausting herself by pitting her strength against his? He must be laughing inwardly at her – or perhaps he was merely filled with the exultancy of the conqueror. 'Let me go,' she pleaded in a very small voice. 'I implore you, Julius—' His lips had released hers long enough for her to say this, but they denied her the time to finish. His kisses were sensuous, demanding and ruthlessly masterful, his eyes dark with the embers of desire, and the glow suffusing Gale's body was fanned into a flame. Was she so easily to be overwhelmed by the heat of his ardour? She would not reciprocate, she vowed fiercely. Julius should not be given the satisfaction of having subdued her to the point where she was mere putty in his hands. 'Let me go,' she begged again, wondering why she bothered, since she was quite resigned to her fate.

'It's too late, Gale; you're asking too much. I would have preferred you to abandon such foolish resistance, but you're far too stubborn, which means that you won't be as happy as I could make you. However, this is how you want it to be—' He broke off as she pleaded again, but instead of listening with any attention he picked her up, standing by the bed a moment, looking into her face. At last he spoke, telling her she was wasting her time. 'You seem to expect the impossible,' he whispered hoarsely. 'You're altogether too tempting, as I told you once before. On that occasion I had to be satisfied with a kiss, but now . . . now, my beautiful Gale, I shall take much more—' Abruptly he stopped, ears alert, his eyes moving from Gale's pallid face to the bathroom door, which was slightly ajar. 'What the devil's happening?' Putting her down, he strode across the room and pushed open the door. Gale followed and they both stood there, staring in disbelief at the great gush of water issuing from the pipe running along one wall of the bathroom.

'A burst,' said Gale unnecessarily and a laugh escaped her, a cracked and faintly hysterical laugh which brought her companion's eyes back to hers.

'How opportune – for you,' he commented tersely, his dark eyes roving over her scantily-clad body as if even now he would snatch a last appreciative glance at her alluring curves. 'Saved,' he said crisply, 'and by so unromantic an incident as a burst pipe!' An enigmatic smile appeared, to hover on his lips. His expression was one of wry humour not unmingled with regret. 'You should be blessing fate for this timely deliverance.' The merest pause. Gravity replacing the humour, he murmured in gentle and subtle tones, 'Are you, my dear?'

Colour rushed to her cheeks at the oblique suggestion that she also experienced disappointment. She was saved the effort of finding some caustic retort by the sudden increase in the flow of water as the gash in the pipe widened. Julius moved swiftly as a stream formed by his feet, but Gale's light slippers were soon soaked. Water continued to pour from the pipe and ran through the bathroom into the bedroom. Julius became brisk, grabbing his dressing-gown and flinging his arms into it.

'I don't suppose you know where the stop-tap is?' And, when Gale shook her head, 'I'd better go and find it, otherwise we're very soon going to be knee-deep in water.'

She stood motionless after he had gone, fascinated by the gushing water and oblivious for the present of the discomfort of wet feet. Why should she feel like this — sort of empty and suspended in limbo? That ancient pipe over there had proved to be her salvation and she was inordinately relieved . . . or was she? With swiftly rising colour she recalled Julius's subtle insinuation, then instantly put it from her. Of course she was relieved by the timely intervention of fate. . . . And yet why wasn't her relief more satisfying? – her mind and body more relaxed? Twisting her head as Julius returned, she noted the heavy frown that had settled on his brow.

'The damned tap must be outside.' He appeared unaware of the fact that she had not moved since he left the room as, thumbing towards the door, he added, 'Buzz off while I get dressed. And when you're dressed you can busy yourself in the kitchen. You'll find bacon and eggs in the fridge; I brought them with me. And you had better fill up a few containers before I turn the water off.'

'Yes, I'll do that.' For one profound moment their eyes met, and Julius laughed.

'Off you go,' he ordered good-humouredly, and she made a move then, out of the room, closing the door softly behind her.

Over an hour passed before they sat down to breakfast, having spent almost half that time mopping up the water and hanging the rugs outside to dry. They sat at a small table in the kitchen, facing one another as they ate the bacon and eggs which Gale had prepared.

'And she can cook as well,' observed Julius with some amusement. 'I usually find that the beautiful ones are pretty helpless when it comes to domesticity.' Reaching for the condiment set, he helped himself to pepper and salt.

'You mean,' Gale could not resist saying, in distinctly acid-sweet tones, 'that mostly you are compelled to go without your breakfast?'

He glanced at her, the glimmer of amusement in his eyes deepening.

'A bite as well, eh? As a matter of fact it might surprise you to know that I'm not a bad cook myself.'

'It certainly does surprise me.' Gale was now in a state of fully restored confidence and she gave him smile for smile. 'I always believed Greek men considered themselves far too superior to indulge in what for centuries has been considered woman's work.'

'In general that is correct; Greek men do consider themselves superior.' Picking up the toast-rack, he held it out to her. Gale helped herself and thanked him.

'You're a strange man, Julius.' Gale spoke after a small silence during which he had sparingly spread butter on his toast while she had merely sat and watched him. 'Have you never had any desire to marry?'

He looked up.

'The desire to marry comes only with the appearance of the right woman.'

'So obviously you've not met the right woman yet.'

'A brilliant conclusion,' he could not help saying, and enjoyed her discomfiture as she blushed at his mild sarcasm.

'I suppose that was a rather stupid thing to say,' she admitted, concentrating on her food.

'What about you? Are you quite determined never to marry?'

'Quite.'

'A decision reached solely because one man let you down. Very silly, Gale; all men are not alike.'

She hesitated a while and then, with sudden decision,

'Father's letting Mother down all the time. Also, I could mention several broken marriages among people I know.' She shook her head. 'It isn't worth the risk.'

'I agree with you that marriage is a risk,' said Julius quietly, and a little gravely, she noticed. 'But if one is exceedingly careful, searching well before allowing oneself to fall in love, then marriage can undoubtedly be the ideal state in which to live.'

Gale stared at him in surprise. So serious he was now – far, far different from the man who only a short while ago had such mischief in mind. Lightly he had meant to seduce her, and just as lightly he could have said good-bye – unless of course she had agreed to continue the affair, as he had hoped, apparently. How long would it have lasted? Perhaps a month or two, or perhaps a year at most. Supposing she had agreed; would she have emerged from it heartwhole? Gale found herself shirking the answer, a circumstance which in effect *was* an answer although she refused to acknowledge it.

'You,' she began, sweeping him a glance from under her long curling lashes, 'You, Julius – would you like eventually to enter into this idealistic state of which you talk?'

His fine lips curved even while his eyes remained grave. Gale owned to herself that this serious mood was enormously attractive.

'You're asking me if I'd like to be married?'

She nodded, a smile fluttering.

'Yes, as a matter of fact I was asking that.'

A moment's silence followed; Julius was deep in thought, and for no definable reason Gale's mind went back to the night of the barbecue and with a dart of memory she heard her brother saying,

'Our Greek friend seems to be affected by your beauty; he hasn't taken his eyes off you the whole evening.'

Desire, obviously, nothing more, Gale now decided, lifting her eyes to glance at him across the table.

'I must admit that until a short while ago I hadn't given much thought to the idea of marriage—' He broke off and for one fleeting second his lips curved in contempt. 'A man doesn't really need to these days – when women are so cheap. If he should desire a woman he can almost always have her without much trouble.'

'You're certainly outspoken,' swiftly and with an edge to her voice. And her violet eyes glinted as they continued to meet his. A moment's hesitation followed and then, unable to resist it, she said, 'You find women boringly easy to – er – conquer, I believe?' and naturally he gave a start, the knife he had been using idle in his hand.

'Where did you hear that?'

'You don't know?' she inquired sweetly. 'Then you must be in the habit of repeating it.'

A dangerous gleam entered his eyes. He said softly,

'I asked you where you'd heard it?'

'At the barbecue,' she admitted after a small pause during which she admonished herself for speaking about the matter at all.

'I see,' he murmured thoughtfully, and added on a note of perception, 'It was not all you heard me say?'

Gale flushed in spite of her challenging air and inner determination not to allow this man to disconcert her.

'No,' she confessed quietly, 'it was not all I heard you say.'

Julius fell silent, his eyes flickering in a preoccupied kind of way. His voice held censure when at last he spoke.

'Are you in the habit of eavesdropping?'

Her flush deepened.

'I had no idea you two were on the other side of the rose hedge,' she returned defensively.

'But having discovered we were, you remained, in order to listen?' Glinting expression and a crisp edge to his voice. His mouth when he stopped speaking became stern and compressed. Gale noted the cold austerity of his features and thought how very Greek he looked at this moment, with his dark skin, and eyes that were almost black.

'I couldn't help hearing some of what was being said. But I didn't deliberately stay there in order to hear more—'

'You heard enough, apparently?' It was a subtle question and Gale looked down at her plate wondering what he would say next. 'You heard me say I'd prefer a fight?' Gale nodded and he then asked, 'And you also heard what came next?'

She looked at him, remembering with vivid force that, just a short while ago, he had managed to place his hand on her heart.

'Your boast was pompous and arrogant, and not what one would expect of a gentleman.'

He smiled then, in some amusement.

'It was man's conversation, remember, and not meant for woman's ears.'

Her eyes swept him with quick contempt.

'Men are despicable the way they talk together about women!'

'Don't women talk about men?'

'Not in the same way. You are always boasting about your conquests, and declaring that women are frivolous and – and lacking strength of character,' she added, trying to recall the Professor's exact words.

'We only speak the truth,' and, when she remained silent, 'If you heard all that it must have been a most unpleasant few minutes you went through.'

'I was furious,' she admitted, glaring at him and receiving only a smile of amusement for her trouble. 'I could have come round there and told you both what I thought about you.' With an angry movement she picked up the coffee pot and added, 'Do you want some more?'

He nodded, his eyes on her flushed face.

'Thank you, Gale.' There was a pronounced alteration in his tone as he added, 'I'm sorry you overheard all that; it's given you a bad impression of me.' Half question half statement. She said crisply,

'Does my opinion of you matter, Julius?'

'Perhaps you won't believe me, but it does.'

Suspiciously she eyed him as the coffee pot was returned to its stand.

'You didn't worry about such things just now, when her words, but there wasn't really any delicate way you tried to – to—' She stopped, in order to re-phrase of putting it and what she eventually did say only made him laugh. 'When you began trying on your tricks.'

'I must admit that my mind was occupied with matters very different from concern about your opinion of me,' he owned with candour, his laugh reflected in his eyes. Gale merely sent him a speaking glance which to her chagrin seemed to afford him a mild sort of pleasure not untinged with satisfaction. Perhaps he was concluding that *her* mind had been similarly occupied by matters far removed from anything even remotely akin to the prosaic. 'What an unromantic climax it turned out to be,' he continued, his expression a mixture of amusement and regret. 'What makes it all so much more vexatious is that you were there, in the other bedroom – all night. What a missed opportunity!'

Her suspicions returned, this time for a totally different reason from that of a moment ago.

'Obviously you're teasing me, Julius, and this makes me wonder if you really were intending the mischief you threatened ... or were you merely trying to frighten me?'

At that the dark eyes opened very wide.

'My dear Gale,' he said in tones of smooth candour. 'My intentions could not have been more dishonourable. I've told you more than once that you're tempting – and that means desirable. I could not possibly have let you leave without learning more about your charms.' He stopped and slanted her a warning look. 'This time you were saved by that damned burst, but should there ever be another occasion when such an opportunity comes my way, then you can be sure you'll not escape a second time.'

'It's most unlikely that there'll ever be another occasion such as this,' she retorted with confidence, and Julius nodded in agreement. 'You haven't answered my question about marriage,' she reminded him, anxious to veer the subject into slightly less personal lines.

'Ah, yes. I was saying that I hadn't given it much thought until recently.' He stopped and she was surprised to discover that he appeared to be searching for words. She was even more surprised to learn that he did not find them, for he merely said, without much expression, 'Let's change the subject, Gale. My marriage prospects can't be of any interest to you.' And he allowed his eyes to flicker over her, in an indifferent sort of way, before giving his full attention to his breakfast.

CHAPTER FOUR

HAVING emerged from her escapade with nothing more serious to remember than her failure to punish apparent when, in a letter to Tricia, he denounced her within a reasonably short space of time. That Trevis had learned all about the attempt to frame him was apparent when, in a latter to Tricia, he denounced her conduct, saying she need not deny hatching the plot as there was no one else to do so. He went on to say that the girl at the lodge was obviously a friend and if ever he should find out who she was it would be the worse for her. Gale merely shrugged the threat from her mind, since she could not visualize any way at all in which Trevis could be revenged on her.

'Just imagine his writing like this.' Tricia was tearful and unhappy as she read the letter to her friend. 'So cold and – and accusing.'

'Isn't that to be expected?' Gale felt forced to ask. 'He's been tackled by Louise's father, and although he was fortunate enough to miss what was planned for him it's only natural that he should be angry over it. I don't suppose you'll hear any more about it, though,' she added in a tone of absolute confidence.

'I'm glad he doesn't know who it was,' said Tricia with a frown. 'It seems he could be vindictive after all.'

Gale said nothing, being indifferent because she could not see Trevis bothering his head about the matter, and in any case there was not the remotest possibility of his discovering who had been at the lodge, for Julius would never divulge her name. Gale was confident of this, since whatever his morals Julius had about him a gallantry that could not be denied. Moreover, he had returned to Greece and Gale had heard from her brother that he was not expecting to be back in England until the late autumn, which was roughly three months ahead, and by this time Trevis would most likely be married and have forgotten all about the episode in which he himself was to have been the chief actor.

And so it was with a sort of astounded disbelief that, only a week later, Gale was listening to her mother telling her that she had received a telephone call from Tricia's fiancé, who had informed her that her daughter had spent the night with a foreigner at the fishing lodge in Cumberland.

'Is this true?' Mrs. Davis looked as if ten years had been added to her age. 'You were away from home on the night in question, having told me you intended staying with one of your colleagues at her cottage in the country.' Mrs. Davis looked probingly into her daughter's eyes, a haunted expression on her face.

'I – I—' Gale stopped, moistening her lips, for her mouth had gone dry, making speech difficult. Never had she visualized a repercussion such a this. Had she even dwelt for a second on the idea that her mother would come to hear of the escapade Gale would have refused instantly to fall in with Tricia's plan. How had Trevis discovered her name? No amount of brain-searching would provide an answer and Gale wondered if it would remain a mystery. She looked at her mother, noted the near-anguish in her tired and pallid face, and without further hesitation she decided that the only way open to her was to tell the truth, even though it meant relating a story that must surely shock her mother. 'It would be useless to lie,' she said, 'but it isn't as bad as it appears. I occupied one room and Julius another—'

'Julius?' interrupted Mrs. Davis swiftly. 'Julius Spiridon – a Greek?' and when Gale nodded uncomprehendingly, 'Edward mentioned him, saying he had been giving you plenty of attention at the barbecue. Edward said he couldn't take his eyes off you.'

'That hasn't anything to do with this business at the lodge—'

'It must have. You stayed there with this Greek, you've just said so.'

'Not *with* him, not in the way you're suggesting, Mother. We occupied separate rooms.' Her mother would have interrupted again, but Gale went on quickly to relate the whole story, fully expecting to see at least some slight relaxing of the strained, tensed features, but instead she saw to her amazement that an expression akin to horror was slowly spreading over her mother's face. 'You don't believe a word of it,' she gasped, realizing only now just how unconvincing her story must sound.

'I don't know how you dare sit there and talk such rubbish to me!' Mrs. Davis ended on a small sob, continuing after a moment, but murmuring to herself rather than to Gale, 'You're your father's daughter . . . and after all my prayers that you would never take after him. A liar – oh, yes, he's told me some lies too, in his time – to account for his nights away from home. but never has he made up a story like this. A liar and a reprobate he's always been, but life was bearable while I had you – and Edward, of course. And now you've also let me down. . . .'

She was still talking to herself, remote from her daughter, who could only stare, shocked by what her mother was saying. She had expected to be scolded for an action which Julius had put down as criminal – and rightly so, Gale now admitted. Yes, she had fully expected a scolding for that, and she had steeled herself to accept it without so much as a word in her own defence. But never had she expected her mother to behave in this way, refusing to believe her, classing her as no better than her father.

'To go and sleep with a man – and a Greek at that!' Mrs. Davis looked up; and Gale flinched at her expression, biting her lip till it hurt. 'How long have you known him?' Her mother shook her head as she spoke and continued without affording Gale an opportunity of replying to her question, 'It can't be long, because you've never even mentioned him.' A great shuddering sigh escaped her. 'To sleep with a stranger—'

'I did not sleep with him!' Anger rose within Gale even while remorse was her chief emotion. That she could have brought suffering to her mother, whom she had always dearly loved. The knowledge brought an almost physical pain to Gale's heart. 'You must believe me; I've told you the truth.'

But Mrs. Davis was shaking her head and Gale's spirits sank into her feet. How could she get the truth through to her mother? She tried, persevering for a long while, her emotions alternating between angry frustration and profound distress at hurting the one she loved best in all the world.

'Is there any possibility of marriage between you?' her mother inquired at last, just as if Gale had not been pleading desperately for over half an hour. 'Or is it merely an affair, indulged in for nothing more than lust?'

Gale flinched, and replied that there was no question of marriage as she and Julius were not even friends. They were merely acquaintances, she said, and even tried again to make her mother accept that there had been nothing wrong between her and Julius.

'It isn't any use,' said Mrs. Davis wearily. 'You're lying all the while; perhaps you don't know it, but you've been blushing all the time you've been talking about this man, and denying there was anything between you.'

Blushing. . . . Yes, she had felt her colour rise – and that was owing to the memory of Julius's intended mischief. Had he not been prevented from carrying out his intentions then Gale's story would have been very different. Yes, she *had* blushed, and this circumstance had served to weaken further a story that already lacked conviction.

'I can never forgive you,' Mrs. Davis was saying bitterly. 'I think I could have done so had you both had marriage in mind, simply because times have changed since my day and it's normal now to be intimate before marriage. Yes, I could have accepted the situation . . . but to think that you knew when you went there that you'd never marry the man!'

Further efforts on her part being useless, Gale left her mother and went out, driving her car into the country, and endeavouring to steal some of the peace she found there. But her mind was in chaos, and her heart ached for her mother. Edward had always prophesied that she, Gale, would one day regret her way of life, but Gale had laughed, confident that she would always be master of any situation in which she found herself. But this situation had been very different from all the rest . . . in more ways than one. . . .

The tantalizing question of Trevis's informant remained with Gale, and the only person she could think of was Julius; but he was not in England. Julius . . . of the attractive iron-grey hair and noble commanding personality. From the first meeting Gale had felt something – indefinable and unreal as the threads of a dream on the awakening, but present all the same. And what of that morning at the lodge? Could she have resisted him? His strength would have overcome any physical struggles on her part, but defeat did not always mean total surrender. What worried Gale, even though she had come safely out of the danger, was that she might just have been forced into total surrender . . . by the charms of the man and by her own feelings regarding him. To admit to his devastating attractions, to own that he moved her at all even, must surely weaken her resistance when the time came for him to exert his persuasive and experienced tactics. She had vehemently declared her innocence to her mother – but was she innocent? Fate alone had saved her, but even now, in all honesty, Gale had to admit that the feeling of emptiness following her escape had a certain element of disappointment about it. And as this admission filled her with shame she tried to shift her thoughts into other, less embarrassing channels.

Yet what else could she think about? It was natural that the whole miserable business recurred over and over again. Julius continued to dominate the scene. She reflected once more on her brother's assertion that Julius could not take his eyes off her; and yet, later when they were talking, Julius had declared that she would have waited till hell froze before she could have affected him with her charms. This obviously meant that he was impervious to these charms . . . and yet he had kissed her, saying he had wanted to do so from the moment he first saw her.

What a strange man – but then he was from the East and, cultured as he was, having been educated in England, he still possessed those inherent traits which were so vastly different from those possessed by people from the West. His temperament was different, and his appearance. He had all the fire of the average Greek's passionate nature, and this was allied to the possessiveness that was traditional, and had been since the ancient times of the pagan gods. A Greek possessed his woman – she was his property, his chattel; she obeyed absolutely his commands, because this also was traditional; she had completely to succumb in every way to her husband's desire and to remember always that his word was law.

What an outdated structure, thought Gale, dwelling for a space on two things Julius had said to her, the first being that the desire to marry comes only with the appearance of the right woman and the second being that until a short time ago he had not given much thought to marriage. That surely must mean that the idea of marriage was now present Gale found herself frowning heavily at the thought of Julius marrying . . . but why should it affect her? His life and the way he chose to live it was no concern of hers. She had endeavoured to pursue the subject, she recalled, but Julius had abruptly changed it, leaving her guessing.

She had stopped the car and got out to walk along the tree-lined lane, but now she turned back and drove home. As usual her father was out, but to Gale's surprise her mother was also out and Gale's heart turned over as she fell to wondering where she could be, for she was always at home in the evenings; in fact, she went out only to shop, and that for about an hour or so – no longer, not usually. Had the behaviour of Gale anything to do with her going out? A troubled frown knitted Gale's brow. Where could her mother have gone?

Ten minutes later Gale found the note; it had been

left on the sideboard, but the opening of the door when Gale entered must have caused a draught and the note had blown on to the floor where it settled just underneath the sideboard, and Gale saw it only when she sat down.

'Don't wait up for me, I shall be late,' was all she read, blinking at the brevity and cold abruptness of the words. Her nerves fluttered uncomfortably, but as there was nothing she could do she determinedly forced herself to be calm. Her mother had mentioned a film that was showing at the big cinema in town; perhaps she had gone there.

But when she did come in she refused to tell Gale where she had been.

'I told you not to wait up for me,' she almost snapped. 'Why did you?'

Gale looked at her, sure she must be ill, as she had never spoken to her daughter in such a tone before.

'I was worried, naturally. You never go out and I couldn't think where you could be.'

'No, I never go out, do I? Well, I shall be doing so in future, and neither you nor your father need inquire about where I go!' and with that parting shot she left Gale standing there, and went upstairs to her room. Gale waited for her father, who made his appearance at half past two in the morning.

'What the dickens ails you?' he demanded in a throaty voice, and then, as the thought occurred to him, 'Your mother – she's not ill, or anything?'

'Would you care if she was?' in a cold tone as Gale examined his face. He'd been drinking – but not until this time of the morning.

'What's up?' he asked briefly, walking towards the couch.

'Mother's been out this evening, and she didn't get

home until after twelve.'

Her father frowned.

'Where did she go?'

'She wouldn't say.' A small hesitation before Gale resignedly told her father of what had transpired earlier. 'I'm sure it was that which caused her to go out,' she ended contritely.

'You went off to Cumberland and stayed with a Greek?' Her father flung back his head and laughed. 'A chip off the old block, eh—?'

'Stop it!' she cried, stamping her foot to give emphasis to her words. 'I've just told you the truth!'

'But your mother didn't believe you?'

'I've told you that too.'

'Neither do I believe you,' he said with a sly grin as his eyes swept over her slender figure. 'Hope you knew what you were about— All right, all right; there's no need to boil up like this. What's wrong with a little fun, anyway? Trouble with your mother is that she's always been too damned strait-laced.'

Gale's violet eyes glinted; she could have struck her father, wiping that grin from his face.

'Strait-laced, is she? What would you say if she began doing what you're doing?'

His mouth went tight instantly and an ugly expression settled on his face.

'Where could she have been until that time of the night?' he asked harshly, and Gale's contempt grew. He himself could play his wicked game, but his wife must remain 'strait-laced', even though he spoke of the term in such derisive tones.

'I've already said, she refused to tell me where she'd been.'

'She doesn't know anyone. I mean, she couldn't have been in a neighbour's house, because she never mixes with the neighbours.'

Gale shook her head.

'No, she'd never go into a neighbour's house.' Her mother was polite, and friendly, but far too reserved go go further than passing the time of the day or making the necessary inquiry when anyone was ill, or there was a birth or a wedding. 'I'm dreadfully worried about her,' Gale went on when her father remained thoughtfully silent. 'She was so upset by what I'd done – by what she believed I'd done, and I'm sure that was the reason she went out.'

'She probably walked about,' her father submitted after a pause. 'Yes, she's that type; she'd wander through the streets, thinking and brooding. She used to do that a long while ago, before either you or Edward were born.'

'She wandered about – all on her own? Why?'

He shrugged carelessly.

'Because of my wicked ways,' he blatantly admitted.

'You were like that, so early in your married life?' Disgustedly she looked at him, but he met her gaze, unashamedly.

'Your mother and I are not suited – never have been from the start—'

'She had two children,' snapped Gale, her eyes blazing.

'What's that to do with it? Cold women can have children.'

Gale swallowed. She hated this conversation, and yet she continued it by saying,

'What you should have had is a harem.'

He only laughed at that and said he agreed with her.

'All men should have more than one wife,' he continued, ignoring the scorn on his daughter's face. 'The people of the East can teach us a lot. Take the Anatolian peasant – he can have four wives. It's so sensible.'

Gale allowed her glance to rake him from head to foot, acutely conscious of the fact that never before had she and her father had such a conversation as this. Both had deliberately steered clear of bringing into the open what they knew was there. But now all pretence was down; her father was not disinclined to talk, while she felt she ought to listen, discovering more about her parents' married life. And as he spoke of things long past Gale's heart went out to her mother with even deeper feeling than before. To live with a man so long, to bear him two children, and be faithful while he basely flaunted all that was sacred in marriage. . . . Her mother had been a saint; Gale saw that now.

'I'd have left you long ago,' said Gale when he had finished speaking. 'I'd have left you to go your own way.'

'You would, yes, but not your mother.' Such confidence in his tone, and Gale's mouth compressed. 'Your mother will be with me till the end; she's made that way.'

'And you – are you intending to continue like this indefinitely?' Gale spoke after a long pause, during which she digested what her father had said, finally agreeing with him. Her mother would stay with him to the end.

'Until I'm too old for—' He broke off and the grin returned. 'Until I'm old, and then we'll settle down, your mother and I, to a happy and peaceful old age.'

'Mother must wait until she's old before she can be happy?' Gale automatically shook her head. 'Can't you change, Father? You must have loved her once.'

'Once? I still love her.'

'You—! Don't be ridiculous! You can't possibly love her.'

'You don't understand, Gale. There's no doubt about my loving her.'

She frowned, bewildered and still disbelieving.

'And yet you leave her, night after night? If I didn't stay in with her three or four times a week she'd be alone every night of her life.'

Her father yawned; he was no longer interested in the subject and as he leant back against the couch she saw his eyelids droop.

'We'd better go to bed,' she suggested, rising from her chair.

'You haven't told me why you stayed up,' he said, stifling another yawn.

'It was to tell you about Mother. I was dreadfully concerned because I couldn't think where she could have gone to.'

'Well, you know now. She just wandered about the streets—' He wagged a forefinger at Gale. 'And this time it's you who are to blame for upsetting her. If you must go off and enjoy yourself in that way then for the lord's sake keep it dark.'

'I did not enjoy myself in that way, as you term it!'

'Come off it, Gale; there's no need to pretend with me. You know very well I'd never blame you—'

'You're despicable!' she flashed and, turning on her heel, she left him sitting there, on the couch, looking ready to fall asleep.

CHAPTER FIVE

When her mother had threatened to go out in future Gale had naturally believed the words to be spoken in the heat of the moment, and expected her mother's normal routine to continue as before. But contrary both to her daughter's expectations and those of her husband, Mrs. Davis continued to go out about four times a week, and no amount of inquiry on Gale's part or threats on her father's would bring from her what she was doing with her time.

'Where can she be going?' This was the third week and Mr. Davis was furiously angry. 'She's like a clam!'

Troubled as she herself was, Gale was stung into saying,

'You've no grumble. Do you ever tell Mother where you've been?'

His eyes kindled.

'If I thought for one moment she was with a man. . . .'

Contempt flashed in his daughter's eyes.

'If she does have a man friend – has it really anything to do with you?'

'I'm her husband,' he shouted in answer to that, and Gale's eyebrows lifted a fraction.

'Isn't it a bit late to remember that?'

He glared at her, crimson colour fusing his face.

'Cynical as ever, aren't you? Well, miss, just because you've a private war on against all men it doesn't mean that you're going to aid and abet your mother in rebellion against me. If I thought for one moment she was with a man,' he said again between his teeth, 'I'd strangle her!'

'You make my blood boil! She must lead a blameless life while you yourself carry on the way you do? I don't know how you have the nerve to talk like this!' Temper was high; nevertheless, Gale's chief emotion was anxiety, for it did seem that her mother had a man friend. And as it would be too much of a coincidence that some man should have conveniently turned up three weeks ago Gale could not help wondering if her mother had previously met someone she could care for, but whom she had resolutely kept at a distance owing to her own high ideals of fidelity. And now, convinced that her daughter had let her down, as her husband had been doing for years, she had thrown ideals to the winds and was herself indulging in an affair.

'I've a good mind to follow her!'

Gale slanted her brows.

'Mother might be simple – by your standards – but she's not so simple that she'd allow you to follow her.'

Mr. Davis went out at last, after repeatedly glancing at the clock. Plainly he had a date, thought Gale, her contemptuous gaze following him as he went past the living-room window on his way to the garage. How many times had her mother ridden in that car? Gale estimated they could be counted on one hand. The car disappeared with unnecessary noise and Gale sat down on the couch, brooding over her mother's changed ways and the rift which had resulted from Gale's own action in going to the lodge and remaining there the night. Mrs. Davis had scarcely spoken to her daughter during the past three weeks, so the atmosphere in the house was one of tension, with man and wife not speaking, mother and daughter speaking only when necessary, and father and daughter quarrelling every time they found themselves alone.

Gale felt she could not endure it much longer and she had in fact already considered changing her job – going to work at the other side of town and sharing a flat with a friend who rented one which was too large for her. But although the idea appealed one moment she flung it aside the next. Her mother would be even more unhappy if she went; and in any case, Gale was ever telling herself that this phase in their relationship would be bound to pass, and the old comradeship would then be resumed. If only she knew what her mother was doing, though. She must be *somewhere*!

Gale's melancholy reflections were abruptly broken into by the ringing of the doorbell and she went into the hall to see who it was.

'Julius!' she gasped, stepping back immediately upon opening the door. 'What—?'

Smiling urbanely, he said, eyes flicking over her as if he just could not help stealing an admiring glance,

'May I come in? You're quite alone, so we can have a nice friendly chat.'

She frowned at him, uncomprehendingly. But she stood aside and gestured; he passed her and she closed the door.

'In here.' Gale pushed open the living-room door and he preceded her into the large, tidy apartment. 'Please sit down.'

'Thank you. Will my car be all right out there – on the road?'

'Of course.' She felt awkward in spite of her innate confidence. But then both she and he were dwelling on what had happened the last time they met. 'Why are you here, Julius? I understood you were not coming to England for some time yet?'

'You didn't ask me how I knew you were alone,' he remarked, ignoring what she had said.

'I expect I was too taken aback by your appearance to grasp what you said. How did you know I'd be alone?'

He said, a pleasant smile hovering on his lips,

'Your mother told me.'

'My—!' She gave him a startled glance. 'When have you seen my mother?'

'Several times lately—'

'But – have you been in England all the time?' Gale eyed him suspiciously and digressed for a moment, asking in a very soft voice, 'Did you tell Trevis that I was at the lodge that night?'

His wide staring gaze was censure in itself and she lowered her lashes.

'I don't know Trevis,' curtly and with the accent more pronounced, the result of anger. 'And if I did, do you honestly believe I'd tell him about your being at the lodge?'

She shook her head, but went on to say,

'Someone told him.'

'We'll come to that later,' he decided crisply. 'The important issue is that you've shocked your mother by your wicked ways – but of course you're aware of this. She's given you her opinion in no uncertain terms, I believe?'

She looked across at him before sitting down on a chair facing the window.

'Hadn't you better begin at the beginning?' she invited, crossing one slender leg over the other and leaning back in a manner of deceptive ease. The last rays of sunlight fell on to her face and hair, highlighting contours and colours. Her violet eyes were wide and curious, her full wide mouth slightly open – invitingly.

Julius's attention was wholly with the lovely picture she made and on noting his changing expression she felt the blood rush to her cheeks, warming them rosily. He smiled to himself and . . . could it be imagination, she wondered, or was there actually a gleam of triumph in those dark disturbing eyes? She swallowed, recalling with stark clarity that scene in the bedroom before the anticlimax of the burst pipe. She had been left in a void of – of . . . Was it really disappointment? At the time the question had risen, and been shelved, but now. . . . The man sitting there was still intently watching her and she lowered her head, hoping it was not too late to conceal her thoughts but very much afraid that the astute Greek would miss nothing.

'At the beginning,' he mused at length, his strong angular features settling into thoughtful lines. 'Where does one begin, I wonder?' However, he immediately went on to explain. Gale learned that her mother had cabled the message that she wanted to see him. 'I came over at once,' he said, and continued, 'Your mother is heartbroken—'

'Only because she absolutely refuses to believe my story,' cut in Gale indignantly.

'Can you blame her?' he queried with a hint of sardonic amusement. 'It entirely lacks credibility.'

'It does not!' she retorted angrily. 'How can the truth lack credibility?'

'Let's get back to where we were,' he said quietly. 'Your mother's heartbroken because, she says, you've taken after your father.'

'You mean – Mother told you all about my father?' She stared at him in disbelief.

'I'm sure she didn't tell me all,' he rejoined with humour, 'but she did tell me sufficient for me to understand how she came to be feeling as she did about you.

She tells me the only thing that will restore her peace of mind is marriage. She can forgive your – er – indiscretion if I make an honest woman of you. Rather antiquated, I must confess, but while your mother's generation is with us these ideals will remain.' He spoke with such unruffled calm – without expression almost – that Gale could only stare in stupefaction for a while, trying to dismiss the incredible idea that was crowding in on her mind.

'Why have you come here?' she managed at last, and Julius lifted one eyebrow admonishingly as he replied,

'This air of mystification is out of character, Gale. You know full well why I've come.'

'I think I must be dreaming.' Dazedly she shook her head, but her heart was acting strangely – beating far too rapidly. Julius laughed and assured her that she was very wide awake. 'Then you are quite mad,' she declared, and again he laughed. How inordinately handsome, with that laugh crinkling the corners of his basalt eyes, and that thick grey hair – so dark, like iron for the most part but a little lighter at his temples so that there was an attractive contrast with his brown skin. Gale braked her thoughts and waited for him to speak.

'What is your answer?' he asked, and leant back, stretching out his long legs in front of him.

'I'd like to hear the question first.'

'Romantic? But you always gave me to understand that you weren't.' Humour lit his eyes, and he paused a moment, absorbed in her expression which was one of derision at his use of the word romantic. 'Will you marry me, Gale?' he ended briefly.

In this unreal situation there seemed to be only one course: to laugh the whole thing off. But Gale knew this was no laughing matter; Julius was in deadly earnest. He had come here especially to propose marriage to her – but surely not merely to mollify her grieving parent?

'I'm interested in the reason for this sudden proposal?' she said at last.

'Damned cool customer you are, Gale – and I like you for it.' Several seconds elapsed as he regarded her with distinct admiration. 'I wonder if any woman has received a proposal of marriage with more cool composure than you?'

'Not this sort of a proposal,' she responded with a certain amount of pride.

'I should imagine these circumstances are unique, and that no woman has ever found herself in your position.'

She had nothing to say to this and for a short spell her mind was busy with reflections of comments Julius had made on various occasions. She was tempting and desirable. Perhaps the most significant remark had been that concerning marriage. He hadn't given it much thought until recently, he had said. Until recently . . . Until he met her? Incredible as it seemed Gale knew it was true. But of course his only interest in her was the pleasure her body would afford him. Greeks were like that; few of them married for love – and certainly it wasn't love that had prompted this proposal. She said, throwing him a level glance,

'You haven't told me the reason for wanting to marry me.'

'Gallantry,' he rejoined promptly, looking over her shoulder to the trees in the garden outside. 'Greeks put a high value on it,' he added, still avoiding her eyes.

'Rubbish! You don't care a rap for Mother's feelings.'

'No? Then perhaps you have your own ideas as to

why I wish to marry you?'

Gale eyed him without betraying what was in her mind.

'You've deliberately avoided giving me an answer to my question,' she reminded him.

Impatience edged his tones when he said,

'I believe I've given you a perfectly valid reason for my desire to marry you. Your mother is most intense about this whole thing. You're a fallen woman in her eyes—'

'Cut out the humour! And perhaps you'll be a little more explicit about the whole business! Who, for instance, informed Mother of my being at the lodge?'

'That? If you remember, I called you Gale.' Julius gestured with his open palms to indicate that this was explanation in itself, but added, 'That bloke from the big house mentioned this name to Trevis and as your friend Tricia had mentioned you to her fiancé he naturally knew who you were – or at least he had a clue to go on. A few inquiries would soon put Trevis in possession of your surname. For sheer spite he phoned your mother, and hence you and I find ourselves in this mess.'

'Mess?' with a lift of her brows. 'You're not in a mess.'

'Not exactly,' he conceded. 'All the same, I do feel responsible, in some small way, for how your mother is feeling. She and I talked a long while and it was not difficult for me to gather that she has been unhappy for a number of years. Her only comfort seems to have been that which she derived from her two children. She had a most high opinion of you and this escapade of yours has shattered her. As I've just said, nothing will eradicate her hurt except our marriage. I finally promised I'd propose to you.'

Cale's eyes narrowed – an almost unconscious action. But deep down inside she sensed a flaw in this seemingly transparent situation.

'Did it not occur to you to give strength to my story by telling her the truth – that we didn't – didn't – that we occupied separate rooms?' Colour naturally rose, pink colour that fused her cheeks, and she averted her head with swift anger as she noted the gleam of amusement enter his eyes.

'The idea did most certainly occur to me. But I saw at once that it would carry no weight with your mother in the mood she happened to be in at the time. She would undoubtedly have accused me of conspiring with you to deceive her. No, Gale, it would never have worked.'

The flaw remained, in spite of Julius's easy and feasible explanation. For one thing, Gale could not conceive of her mother asking Julius to propose marriage to her daughter. Mrs Davis was by nature exceedingly shy, especially with men ... and Julius Spiridon was not even an ordinary man. His personality would overwhelm a woman of the world, so certainly Mrs. Davis would never have gathered the courage to suggest he marry her daughter. But even if she had, the suggestion should, in the ordinary way, have been flatly turned down. This was the picture as Gale saw it ... but a very different picture had emerged.

'There's a great deal I don't understand,' she sighed at length, glancing up at him and expressing inquiry, even while convinced that he would pass lightly over her puzzlement, which he did.

'It's all quite simple, Gale. Your mother's peace of mind depends on our marriage – because as far as she's concerned we did spend the night together. I'm willing to marry in order that she shall have that peace of mind, and now the rest is up to you.'

She moistened her lips, amazed to feel excitement throb in her veins, astounded to discover that the contemplation of marriage to this god-like Greek with the stern set features presented no distasteful reactions. On the contrary. . . . Colouring, she automatically put a cool hand to one cheek. No use pretending; she desired him even as he desired her. Frail foundation for a marriage. Of course, she had no intention of marrying him; the desire would be extinguished once he and she said goodbye for ever. Or would it . . .?

'I haven't the slightest intention of marrying,' she told Julius at last. 'You know my feelings on the subject; I made up my mind five years ago, and nothing has happened to make me change it.'

Very slightly his jaw tightened. There was no other indication that her answer disappointed him. With smooth urbanity he inclined his head and seemed for a space to accept her decision with equanimity. He even rose from his chair and stood, looking down at her with the merest hint of amusement curving the full sensuous mouth. But then he said, right out of the blue,

'You're obviously unaware of the repercussions this decision will cause. Your mother intends – if I don't make an honest woman of you – to leave you and your father to go your own wicked ways. She will go and live with her man friend.'

An electric silence fell on the room. Gale stared at him in stupefaction, her nerves taut as if ready to snap.

'This isn't true,' she whispered at last, white to the lips. Her mother . . . to do *that*! Impossible! 'My – my mother hasn't got a man friend.' Forced words; Gale had known all along that her mother must be meeting a man. 'And – and if she had,' continued Gale inconsistently, 'she wouldn't tell anyone about it. And she'd *never*, *never* live with a man. Why, you've just said yourself that she has ideals about such things.' Gale's face was still drained of colour. She couldn't see Julius lying about so profound a matter as this. 'She's always been horrified at people flaunting their immorality the way they do.'

Julius glanced at his wrist watch.

'I'm afraid I shall have to go. As for your mother and her intentions – I suggest you have a talk to her about them.'

Gale stared through the window for a long while after the departure of the Greek. He seemed in a hurry to leave at the end, yet somehow Gale could not accept that he was forced to go. She felt instinctively that had her answer been what he wanted then he would have stayed with her throughout the entire evening. She now felt lost, drained . . . missed the presence of a man whose desire for her had prompted the offer of marriage, a man whose desire had awakened something in her she had never known before. With self-disgust she tried to crush the truth, to tell herself that women were different from men anyway – they never experienced desire merely by being with a man, in his company. It was only the male of the species that knew these primitive urges.

Getting up from the chair which she had occupied since his departure, Gale went into the kitchen to make herself a cup of tea. Did she think this prosaic action would restore her sanity? Julius Spiridon had aroused certain emotions in her on their very first meeting – the only man to do so since the break with Malcom five years previously. Gale had fully believed herself to be immune; it had come as a shock to discover this immunity could be broken down, by a Greek of all people. But then he was so vastly different from all other men, with that air of superiority and that dictatorial masculinity which she had already admitted could thrill even though it spelled an ability to subjugate entirely.

Taking the tea back to the living-room, she sat down again, musing on what Julius was doing and knowing for sure that he was thinking of her and seeing her in this turmoil of indecision— Indecision? Certainly not! She hadn't the slightest intention of marrying Julius. Why, they would scrap every single moment . . . no, not quite. . . .

She shuddered at her own mind-pictures. What a life – to be in harmony only when they were making love! Gritting her teeth with impatience at her meditations, she put down the cup and saucer and began walking about the room, rather like a caged bear she had once seen at the zoo, she thought, coming to a halt at last. If only her mother would come in, so that she could find out a little more than Julius had told her. But her mother didn't come, and Gale paced the room again, made herself more tea, sat down – and after what seemed an eternity her father's key was heard in the lock and he entered the room where Gale had spent the entire evening, the greater part of it alone, torn by her confusion of mind and her indecision. Yes, she admitted it at last, because in all honesty she was forced to do so. Marriage to Julius. Fiery and emotional life would always be; quarrels and making up – then love. And perhaps in the end each going their own chosen way, simply because there was nothing but the brittle cord of passion to bind them — nothing spiritual, nothing mental, even . . . just a physical attraction that must surely weaken, and finally die owing to lack of other supporting interests which those in love inevitably must share.

'What's wrong with you?' Her father stood in the middle of the room and searched his daughter's face. 'Seen a ghost?'

'Where have you been?' It was the first time she had asked him this and his lips moved, quivering with anger.

'What the devil has it to do with you? Where's your mother?'

She wondered what he would say should she calmly remark, 'She's out with her man friend.' Aloud she said,

'I don't know. I'm waiting for her to come in; I want to talk to her.'

'What about?' Harsh tones and a glance at the oak clock on the wall. It was about to chime the hour of midnight. 'She's up to no good till this time of the night!'

'You've only just arrived home yourself,' Gale flashed, looking him over contemptuously and half inclined to throw wide the door in order to let escape the nauseating odour of stale beer which emanated from his breath and his clothing. Mingling with this was the smell of tobacco – cigarette smoke adhering to his jacket and his hair. Gale fell to wondering what her mother's friend was like and whether he was the clean wholesome type . . . like Julius, who smoked not at all and drank little; who always seemed just to have emerged from a shower; whose shirts were immaculate as his suits. His hair shone always – shone like polished steel, and he used a delightful after-shave lotion which invariably set Gale musing on his island and its mountains and the wild tang of herbs growing there and the pure cool breeze sweeping in from the sea.

'She's no right to be out! I'll wait up with you and give her what for!' He lurched towards the couch and slumped into the cushions.

'You'll not lay a finger on Mother while I'm here!'

'Lay a finger?' His glazed eyes widened. 'Have I ever used violence against your mother?'

Impatiently she drew a long breath.

'Is that anything to your credit?' she asked after a long pause.

'I've always maintained that a man should never use his superior strength to subjugate a female. And I've stuck to that principle, young woman. Though maybe if I'd given you a clip over the ear now and then you wouldn't be so damned impertinent now. You'd not be standing there, like some blasted judge – looking at me in this way. Your own father! Sit down, if you must wait for her to come in!'

'You'd be better in bed. I want to talk to Mother alone.'

'You do? What about?' he demanded again.

'A private matter.' She saw that his eyes were closing. 'Why don't you go up? You can say what you have to say in the morning – when you're feeling better.'

'When I'm sober, you mean?' He laughed at her expression of disgust and then ordered her again to sit down.

'I'm going to bed.' She went out and left him there. But she lay awake, alert in case there was to be a quarrel. Guilt swept through her as she mused on the peace which had reigned before that fateful night when she had decided to pay Trevis out for what he had done to her friend. True, her mother's life hadn't been happy, but at least there had been no strain such as there was now. Gale and her mother would sometimes take a stroll in the park of an evening, or they would sit and talk. Gale used to go out with her friends, of course, but she always made a point of spending two or three nights in with her mother. Her father went his own way, but no sharp words were spoken between him and his wife, and even Gale was so resigned that she accepted his way of life without comment. And now, owing to Gale's own action, there was strife and bickering all round.

She stiffened under the bedclothes as she heard her mother enter the house and close the front door quietly behind her. No sound of voices. Her father was obviously asleep on the couch; nothing short of an earthquake would waken him until the morning. Gale slipped out of bed and reached for the robe hanging behind the door. Softly she went into her parents' room.

'Is something wrong?' Mrs. Davis looked frowningly at her . . . and for some quite incomprehensible reason Gale had the uncanny impression that her mother was acting a part. So many things now about her mother that were both puzzling and disturbing. Gale always believed she understood her perfectly, but lately she was beginning to doubt if she would ever understand her.

'Don't you know what's wrong, Mother?'

Mrs. Davis shook her head, slipping off her coat and opening the wardrobe door in search of a hanger, a satin-covered hanger on which she had spent so much of her time, sitting alone, ruching the satin ribbon and fastening it round the wooden coathanger, making it look pretty. Everyone in the house had these hangers, and so did Edward and his wife.

'I haven't the faintest idea what could be wrong.'

'You don't sound particularly troubled, either.'

'Why should I be? You lead your own life, your

father leads his, and I lead mine. If we have problems then we must solve them ourselves – without the help of others.'

Gale's eyes glinted. She watched her mother carefully hang the coat in the wardrobe, buttoning it up so that it hung straight.

'Julius Spiridon's been here.'

'Oh . . . he said he'd be coming to see you.'

'He tells me you have—' Gale broke off and began again, after a hesitation for the subject was so delicate. 'Is it true that you have a – a man friend?'

Closing the door of the wardrobe and automatically twisting the key in it, Mrs. Davis turned. It suddenly struck Gale that she loked ten years younger – and she looked inordinately pretty. And her dress; it was at least three inches shorter than she normally wore her dresses. Gale's eyes fell to the hem; it had been taken up by hand. Gale blinked. The last thing she could imagine was her mother, sitting down, and deliberately shortening a dress.

'Disgusting!' her mother had said – and that was only when dresses came just above the knees!

'I have a friend, yes—'

'A man friend?'

'A man friend.'

Her daughter gaped; this bald admission staggered her even more than when the information had been imparted to her earlier in the evening by Julius.

'How long have you known him?'

'It isn't any of your business, but I'll tell you all the same. I've known him over three years.'

'Three years!'

'He asked me to go out with him, but I refused. Two wrongs never add up to a right, I told myself. So although your father played his games I did not. Besides,

I had you to think of; I didn't wish to lose your respect. Now, I don't care if I do, because the respect of a daughter like you isn't all that important.'

Gale winced. This was so unlike her mother, and as the silent moments passed, and they stood there looking at each other, Gale felt the pain of tears behind her eyes.

'I never did that thing you believed of me. Julius should have denied it too.'

'He's an honest man, a trustworthy man. Did he ask you to marry him?'

Gale nodded, aware of the sensation that her mother was acting a part. Yet why should she? And what sort of a part was she acting? It all added up to nonsense and Gale dismissed it, although it still hovered in her subconscious and was to come to the fore later, with far-reaching effects.

'Did you tell him that you'd leave Father and me and – and go and live with this – this man, if I didn't agree to marry Julius?'

'I did say that, yes.' So calmly spoken! Was this the mother who hitherto had been so shy and strait-laced, as her husband always described her? Gale found herself staggered into speechlessness and for a space she just shook her head from side to side, wondering if she were dreaming. She said presently,

'You couldn't possibly have meant it.'

'I can't blame you for being sceptical. But I certainly dc mean it. Why should I live in this house with two such immoral people as you and your father? I might as well find pleasure myself as well.'

'Do you love him?'

'I've loved him almost from the moment we met.' A touch of sadness entered the quiet tones; Gale knew a sudden hurt near her heart and for one reckless moment wished her mother the best of luck! But she soon recovered. Her mother mustn't do this thing; she would be bound to regret it quite soon, as guilt must take full possession. Mrs. Davis was made that way.

'You'll give him up if I marry Julius?' Gale watched her mother's face closely. It seemed to pale a little.

'I shall never give him up now, but I'd not go and live with him.'

A profound silence ensued before Gale spoke.

'In other words, you're holding out a threat which is in effect blackmail? Either I marry Julius or you leave us?'

'Call it blackmail if you wish,' returned her mother indifferently. 'I told Julius that your action had destroyed all my ideals. I said that the only thing which would make me feel less bitter was for you to marry him. I did suggest this to you, if you remember?'

'And I told you there was no question of marriage, as Julius and I were merely acquaintances.' Her mother said nothing, merely crossing over to the dressing-table and taking out a tissue from a packet and soaking it in eau-de-Cologne. 'You'd have me marry a man I don't love?' Still no response; Mrs. Davis casually applied the tissue to her face. Gale's mouth went tight. 'I told Julius there was something I didn't understand – and there certainly is! Does it not occur to you that certain aspects of this situation aren't feasible? – that to me they can scarcely ring true? I know you well enough to be sure you'd never wish me to marry a man with whom I'm not in love, one who could never love me?'

At those last words her mother opened her mouth, then closed it swiftly. Undoubtedly words had leapt to her mother's lips, in one unguarded second, only to be caught back just in time. Nerve-ends prickled along

Gale's spine. She had an urge to ask her mother what it was she had been about to say, then realized she would receive no satisfaction whatsoever. If her mother had wanted her to hear the words then she would have spoken them. Sighing heavily and impatiently Gale said, her voice edged with ill-humour, 'There's something very odd going on, something known only to you and Julius.' Had her mother given a start at those words? Gale couldn't be sure and she breathed another impatient sigh. 'I shan't marry him, so that appears to end the whole business.'

Mrs. Davis twisted round to the mirror, took out a dry tissue and dabbed her face dry.

'Then I shall go and live with Jack.'

Embarrassed colour shot into Gale's cheeks, for the mentioning of the man's name seemed to give the affair a stark and nasty flavour of reality.

'I can't believe you mean it, Mother.'

'Then you'll just have to wait and see, won't you?' Mrs. Davis had apparently finished with her toilet, and with the subject, for she said dismissively, 'I'm tired, Gale, and you must be too. Goodnight.'

'But, Mother—!'

'Goodnight, Gale.'

'Is that your last word? You'll really leave Father and me?'

Mrs. Davis swallowed something in her throat; Gale missed the action as she was glancing again at the length of her mother's dress. So old-fashioned she had been, but now. . . . She had shapely legs, Gale saw with surprise – and the tightened belt emphasized a tiny waist and dainty curves above. It suddenly struck Gale that her mother was only forty-four. She had always seemed so old, like a woman in her late fifties.

'It's my last word, Gale. I'm not willing to live with

two shameless immoral people. One is sufficient and if you remain here then I go.'

Unbelievably Mrs. Davis gestured towards the door, telling Gale to close it quietly when she went out, as she preferred her husband to remain where he was for the rest of the night. Gale could only stare, hurt and angry, furious with herself and with Tricia, and with Trevis for being the prime cause of all this. She was even angry with Julius for agreeing to marry her, but, strangely, she was less angry with her mother than with anyone else. She had no idea why, but something told her the reason would come to her at some time or another.

CHAPTER SIX

GALE stood in the shady arched courtyard and frowned at the cold moon that shone over the volcanic landscape – the three mountain masses formed of igneous rocks spewed up countless ages ago as molten magma from the depths of the sea. A breathtaking kind of beauty existed in this barren countryside, differing entirely from the lush hillsides rising from the sandy beach below her husband's arched and terraced house above the village of Chora.

Turning her head, she encountered his meditative gaze, and turned swiftly away again.

'I'm ready to leave when you are,' she informed him icily. 'If you had to turn back you could at least have resisted the temptation to stop and gossip. Or did you keep me waiting on purpose?'

Julius, immaculate in black suit and white shirt, spoke softly, putting his mouth close to her ear.

'Since our marriage a month ago I have repeatedly warned you to be careful how you speak to me. If you are wise, Gale, you'll heed my warnings, for otherwise you're going to find life rather unpleasant.' With a proprietorial hand on her arm he arranged her wrap with the other. Viciously she twisted away, but the grip on her arm brought her round again. 'If we're going to quarrel we'll do it in the car, not in our host's outer courtyard. Even here, we could be heard. Come!'

Gale had no option but to obey, since his grip was obviously not going to slacken until they reached the car, which was standing on one side of a wide drive leading off the courtyard.

'Why did you keep me waiting so long?' she demanded immediately she was in the car and he sitting beside her. 'You were gone more than ten minutes. You said you'd only be a moment!'

'A figure of speech, which you should have accepted as such. One always says one will only be a moment.' The engine purred and the car slid away along the moonlit drive towards the road. 'I had forgotten a small item of business which I had meant to discuss with Adonis and the others—'

'You didn't tell me it was to be a business dinner! I understood it was to be social; I was never so bored in my life with a conversation!'

'You had the women to talk to.'

Gale drew an angry breath.

'What on earth induced me to marry you I'll never know!'

A twist of his head and a fleeting glance; she noted with increasing fury the humorous lift to the corners of his mouth.

'That's a lie,' he told her quietly. 'You are fully aware that you married me for the same reason I married you.'

She went red, but lifted her chin and swiftly denied,

'I did not! I married you because of Mother!'

Julius's laugh rang out. It grated on her nerves, but it was not until he spoke that she knew the reason for the laugh.

'Do you realize what you've admitted? You're so heated inside with anger against me that you speak without thinking. You've just admitted, by your denial, that you did in fact marry me for desire. You wanted me as much as I wanted you; it's always been like that, right from the first. No, don't argue, Gale. Be honest for a change and admit that a woman has the same inclinations as a man.'

'I married you for my mother's sake.'

'You stubborn wretch, Gale. One of these days you're going to try my patience too far!'

'Your threats don't frighten me, Julius. I can stick up for myself.' She spoke with confidence because, contrary to her expectations, Julius had proved to be tolerant rather than firm, understanding rather than impatient. He was inordinately easy to manage after all. He quarrelled, naturally, when she provoked him to extremes, and his warnings came at regular intervals. They were received by Gale with derision simply owing to his lack of a follow-up. He threatened, then appeared to forget all about it, so life with Julius had turned out to be far less stormy than Gale had anticipated when, after days of indecision, she had accepted his proposal of marriage.

Reminiscently she dwelt for a space on the events preceding her decision. Her mother's adamant attitude, her swearing she would go and live with this Jack if Gale refused to marry Julius. Gale had argued until she was, figuratively, blue in the face, argued that her mother had no intention of carrying out her threat. It seemed in the end that she meant what she said. All this time Gale's father went his sublime way, oblivious of the tussle taking place between mother and daughter. He growled at his wife, he swore he'd make her suffer if it was a man she was meeting on these outings of hers, but all this was superficial; he trusted his wife so implicity that what little concern he had at first experienced soon gave way to his former easy-going attitude. He even told Gale that her mother was going out with another woman, and went as far as to say he was glad she had found a companion.

However, despite her mother's continued threats

Gale might still have refused to marry Julius, but on two occasions she had found herself in a position similar to that at the lodge, though not of course so dangerous. The first time was when Julius had called again at the house and, finding Gale alone – as he later said he knew he would – he took her into his arms, laughing at her resistance, and kissed her with the same passion and force as on that occasion in the lodge.

'You'll marry me,' he had told her ardently, making no attempt this time to 'place his hand on her heart'. But he knew just how to arouse her desires and she found herself quivering with nervous tension, intensely affected by his finesse and practised art of lovemaking. His knowledge of his own power was a weapon which took him half way to victory. Assured, confident . . . because of his inordinate attractiveness – his looks, his physique, his experience of women. 'Yes, my lovely, desirable Gale, you'll marry me – because you won't be able to help yourself!' And he had released her then, and stood looking down at her pale face and quivering lips . . . and although she swiftly lowered her beautiful lashes she was nevertheless plunged into confusion by the sure knowledge that he had already glimpsed the cloudiness which his lovemaking had brought to her eyes. He laughed softly, a laugh that told her nothing, and he moved away from her and said prosaically, 'Gale, my sweet, I don't know how you feel, but I could do with a cup of coffee.'

The second occasion on which he had her completely in his power was at a party. Feeling she must have air, Gale managed to slip away, only to be seen by Julius, who followed her into the darkness and quietness of the garden. She could have escaped, she told herself afterwards, could have run back to the house before he even had time to catch her up. She hadn't tried to escape, and once again she knew the attraction of him, an attraction which during the following few moments she admitted was inescapable. Their paths would divide one day, she accepted with resignation, but for the present there was one path only for them both to tread. That path was marriage, since Julius was now determined on this. Previously he would have indulged in an affair; this idea seemed to have faded, but Gale did wonder what her future would have been had he tempted her in this way. Could she have resisted – when she couldn't resist marrying him? As the question had not arisen Gale thrust the matter from her – and she was exceedingly relieved to do so!

Julius was turning the car on to the forecourt outside the low stone villa and Gale was brought back with a jerk to the present. The moon was high, and brilliant as floating ice. Sounds and smells assailed her senses as she got out of the car and straightened up beside the tall lean shape of her husband, standing there, holding the car door open for her.

'The flowers at night are marvellous,' she breathed ecstatically. 'And the cicadas – they're just part of all the magic!' Her whole manner had changed; excitement throbbed till it formed an ache in her heart and her chest. The car door slammed and all was still as Julius lifted her right off her feet and carried her to the verandah where a light had been left on by Apollo, the Greek manservant employed by Julius, and who had sufficed until Gale came. Now there was Katriana – Kate for short – who looked to Gale's needs.

'Shall I carry you right in, and to our room, or do you want some supper?' Triumph in his voice; she hated it, suddenly, and said,

'I want some supper – of course I do.'

He put her down, and regarded her with a sort of

mocking amusement in those dark basaltic eyes.

'Then by all means you shall have some supper, my dear. Delay will give your ardour time to warm up.'

'Or cool off,' she retorted almost before the last word was out of his mouth. Her eyes glinted and she compressed her lips. She had wanted to be pliant and yielding, and surely out there by the car he saw this. Now she had only the desire to be awkward, and coupled with this emotion was a rising self-disgust. This often occurred, and she would picture herself at eighteen – trusting and wildly in love with Malcolm. Spiritual and mental attraction had come first; physical desire had come later, shyly and reluctantly admitted to her consciousness, and then dismissed. Such thoughts must not establish themselves firmly until she and Malcolm were married.

And now she had married for physical desire only. There was nothing else between her husband and herself, not even a pleasant friendship. Perhaps that was because each secretly despised the other, aware as they were of the reason for the marriage. How long would it last? she often wondered. Julius had at the very beginning warned her it was for ever, as he was a Greek and Greeks intensely objected to divorce. So they would just part company when at last their desire reached satiation point, leaving only the dregs of revulsion. Gale shuddered. For the first time she wished she had not agreed to this marriage.

Looking up into the face of her husband, she saw that his eyes glinted at her, but he merely said,

'Shall we go in, and then you can tell Kate what you want for your supper?'

His indifference irritated; she wished he would lose his temper for a change. Quite irrationally she felt she had exhibited awkwardness for nothing, that she'd been cheated, although of what she could not possible have said.

The supper tray was brought in ten minutes later and Gale regarded it with a frown. The dinner she and Julius had eaten at his friend's house had been sumptuous and she had felt at the end that she wouldn't eat again for a week. And now she was obliged to partake of at least one sandwich, and drink the coffee Kate had brought for her.

'Aren't you having anything?' Superfluous question; she was fully aware of it. Julius ate sparingly at any time. Most certainly he'd not eat now.

'Sorry I'm unable to keep you company,' he drawled, lifting a hand to stifle a yawn. 'In fact, if you'll excuse me, I think I'll go to bed.' A light kiss was dropped on her brow and then he was gone. Seething, for no reason she herself could explain, Gale glared at the closed door, then she pushed the tray to one side and sat staring at the food daintily laid on it. How long she stared she did not know, but eventually she rang the bell and told Kate to remove it. The Greek woman stared at the untouched food and drink, shrugged her shoulders slightly, and obeyed the order Gale had given.

It was an hour later that Gale entered the room she and Julius shared. The bed was empty, the covers turned down and her nightdress daintily spread from one pillow downwards, like something displayed in a lingerie shop. Kate always did this; she was artistic, as many Greek women are, and she was equally adept with flowers or leaves, or with the lunch or dinner table. The sight of that nightdress, undisturbed since Kate had put it there this morning, spoke volumes, and to her amazement Gale experienced a sudden lightness of spirit. Julius was sleeping on his own, in the room adjoining this. Her eyes straying to the half-open door, Gale moved towards it. Yes, there he was, fast asleep – breathing evenly and quietly. Let him! And he could continue to sleep on his own. His doing so would at least result in a situation where her self-respect could be restored.

Up before him the following morning, Gale was interested to see how he would behave, how he would greet her and whether he would comment on his action in occupying the other bedroom.

'Good morning, Gale.' Lazy eyes appraised her from head to foot. 'You're up bright and early. Couldn't you sleep?' Humorous crinkles fanned from the corners of his eyes; the sun glinted on the iron-grey hair and on his polished brown skin. Gale had been standing by the rail of the verandah, looking out towards the turquoise sea, smooth as a pond and stretching away to the shores of Asia Minor. A certain peace had enveloped her, and now she frowned inwardly as nerves became taut.

'On the contrary, I slept more soundly than for a while.' She hoped he believed her, hoped she had no give-away traces of the fitful night she had spent, telling herself one moment that she was glad to be alone, and the next admitting that she missed her husband.

'Strangely,' came the pleasantly-modulated tone in response, 'so did I. We must try this new method more often.'

Silence. She glanced down at her fingers, resting on the rail. To one side of her vines climbed a trellis and scrambled over the roof supports of the verandah, providing shade from the brilliant glare of the sun. At the other end of the verandah bougainvillaeas flaunted their violet and orange flowers, as they did on the wall at the far end of the garden, close to which grew lemon and tangerine trees, their fruits resembling outsize gems as they nestled among the shiny green foliage. What was Julius trying to do to her? Gale was asking herself as the wordless hush continued. They must try the new method more often. . . . Last night she had vowed he should continue to sleep on his own . . . yet a few short hours later she was in that restless state of uncertainty. Pretence was dishonest, she now admitted. As Julius had said once: she desired him just as much as he desired her. Pride forced words from her lips which she did not mean.

'An excellent idea, Julius. It's rather more comfortable, you must have discovered? Your climate is so sultry, and added to that both you and I are used to sleeping alone.' She smiled sweetly at him as she spoke, but a trace of acidity edged her voice and another silence ensued, with her husband regarding her with the arrogance she resented and the humour that set her teeth and temper on edge.

'You might be used to sleeping alone, but how can you be so sure that I am?'

She actually gave a start, disconcerted by this sally. Its implication hurt, too, but this she scarcely noticed just at present. What she did notice was a fluttering in her throat and knew that a pulse was throbbing wildly there.

'Your witticisms might be bright, for so early an hour, but they're hardly in good taste.'

'Why? Isn't it the fashion nowadays for husband and wife to talk about their previous affairs?'

'In this case it would be entirely one-sided.'

'So you'd feel cheated?'

Suddenly she glared at him. He had moved and was idly leaning against the corner pillar of the verandah. His very manner, languid and careless, his narrowed regard and the arrogant slant of an eyebrow . . . all these fired her already heightened temper.

'Shall we go in to breakfast?' she snapped. 'It must be ready by now!'

He threw her a glance, deliberately inquiring.

'Are you feeling off-colour, my dear?'

Gale gritted her teeth.

'You're being particularly trying this morning, Julius,' she told him unsteadily. 'What your object is I can't imagine, but I'm not in the mood to spar with you. Sorry if that disappoints you, but there it is, I'm afraid.'

He laughed, moved closer, and before she had time to twist away out of reach he was patting her cheek and saying,

'Retreating, are you? Not at all brave of you. Don't make a practice of it, though, for I rather enjoy our slanging matches; they provide diversions in which could otherwise become a dull existence.' Smoothly spoken words; he appeared indifferent to the startled glance she gave him.

'Dull – already?' A strange fear caught at her throat but remained undetected in her voice. 'Life with me is becoming dull?'

'I said it could become dull.'

She hated his indifference, his calm acceptance of the fact that the romance might very soon wear off.

'You should have considered this aspect before coercing me into marriage!'

'Coercing?' He slanted an eyebrow. 'My dear girl, you were more than willing to marry me.'

'What an opinion you have of yourself!' she flashed in tones of contempt. 'Be careful, Julius, that you don't provoke me too much. There's no love in this marriage, remember. I could just decide to go home.'

A silence fell fleetingly between them. When presently he spoke his voice was tinged with amusement. His manner remained confident; he knew she would never leave him.

'Home to Mother? She'd not have you. She's old-fashioned, remember, and would undoubtedly tell you a wife's place is with her husband.'

'She would?' Gale's eyelids flickered. She spoke in soft and curious tones. 'But Mother intended leaving Father, leaving him for another man.' Briefly their eyes met before Julius glanced away, apparently interested in the pretty gecko which was running along the rail of the verandah. Had she caught him unawares? wondered Gale, waiting for him to speak. His head came round again; she assumed an expression which plainly reminded him that she considered there was still a mystery surrounding the events leading up to the marriage.

'Your mother probably considered she had given her marriage a fair trial – and in any case, she had an excuse for leaving your father. He'd been unfaithful for years.'

'I shall never understand how she came to confide in you the way she did. It's so out of character, for Mother's always been so shy.' Gale spoke reflectively, disgressing as she dwelt on the incredible change which had taken place in her mother since hearing of the incident at the lodge. Gale also dwelt on her previous conviction that her mother had been acting a part, especially on the night she had first threatened to go away with her man friend.

'Sometimes it's easier to talk to a stranger than a member of one's own family, or even a friend,' Julius was saying. 'Your mother appeared to be immeasurably relieved once she had opened up and told me of her troubles.'

'It only adds to the mystery,' murmured Gale almost to herself. And she went on, 'Nothing will ever convince me that she would have gone off and lived with another man. She's too innocent.'

Julius half smiled at the word but made no comment on it.

'If you were so sure of this then you'd no real need to marry me.' A subtle question, but a statement also. Gale flushed, unable to find anything to say to this and after a moment Julius continued, smoothly and in tones which she thought were tinged with contempt, although she could not be sure of this, 'You married me because you knew darned well you couldn't do without me, as I've previously implied. One day you'll be honest and admit it.'

Her blushed deepened at this outspoken declaration, and, unable to deliver a cutting riposte, she took refuge in saying,

'I've just told you, I'm not in the sparring mood this morning. And in any case, I'm ready for my breakfast. Shall we go in?'

Her husband laughed, yet her mind carried the conviction that suppressed anger affected the timbre of his voice as she heard him say,

'Avoiding the issue again, I see. Well, my dear, I'll not torment you,' and he left his comfortable position by the rail and followed her into the house.

Later they went down to the beach and swam together for a while, Julius affable and smiling, and Gale cool as always, her intention being to keep her husband at a distance – for the most part – so that when the time came for them to say goodbye she would experience no unnecessary pangs of regret. Regret . . .? How odd that the idea should even intrude into her mind. With love absent, how could there be regret, once the fire of physical attraction had become a heap of dead ashes?

Gale sat on the sandy beach and gazed pensively at the swimmer far out there – the man who was her husband, the man whose deeply impressive and unusually forceful personality had affected her right from the moment of their first meeting. How strongly he swam! Everything was easy to him. Yesterday the car had gone wrong and without any hesitation he had rolled up his sleeves and probed about under the bonnet. Within twenty minutes or so the car had been running smoothly again. His work, too, appeared to present him with no headaches. He would spend a couple of hours in his study every day after lunch, and always emerge looking perfectly satisfied and untroubled. He would employ himself in the garden now and then, and one day last week he had even taken over the task of cleaning the house windows, as Apollo was away in his native village, attending a wedding which lasted three days.

Gale's interest increased as another swimmer made in a straight line for where Julius was, returning now with powerful strokes which had a deceptive languor about them. The two met in the water; Gale saw the girl shake her head, saw the long golden hair touch the bare brown shoulder of her husband.

They emerged from the water together, walking towards where Gale sat, under the warm sun pouring down on to the soft pale sands. The couple were chatting like old friends; Julius laughed at something the girl said, and he actually tugged her hair in a little playful gesture . . . so unlike anything Gale would have expected of him. She found herself frowning at this act of familiarity and with a flash of retrospection heard Julius admitting he'd had lots of women. Was this one of them?

A few seconds later the two girls were shaking hands, each examining the other with unconcealed interest while Julius, faintly amused at the expression on his wife's face, picked up a towel and began drying himself with it.

'It was such a surprise to hear that Julius was married,' gushed Daphne, one hand idly fingering her lovely hair, which, Gale noticed, was almost silver in places. 'What an unpredictable man he is!' A flashing glance at him as she spoke, her manner one of possessiveness, almost.

'Do you live near here?' inquired Gale in a cool tone, her eyes flickering now over the lovely tanned body of the other girl, who, she guessed, was about twenty-eight years of age. Slender limbs and shapely; curves which would assuredly cause any man to look twice. The girl wore a bikini, as did Gale herself, but whereas Gale's top half revealed very little, Daphne's left practical nothing to the imagination. Dislike welled up within Gale. She never for one moment considered the word jealousy.

'We live in the villa just below Julius's. We've been away for a few weeks, that's why you and I haven't met before now.' For all its surface charm there was a sort of venomous undertone to Daphne's voice, and the glance she now fluttered at Julius was transparently one of blame. 'I go away, leaving my bachelor friend all alone, and return to find him married! Our Greek help told me of this, but I just didn't believe it.'

'No?' with acid sweetness from Gale. 'Well, you have to believe it now, don't you?' Gale avoided her husband's eyes, but instinctively she knew he had glanced sharply and censoriously at her. Daphne deliberately gasped, audibly, so that Julius should hear.

'Have I said something I shouldn't?' she inquired innocently, her big blue eyes taking on a worried look. 'Julius, do tell me if I've been – er – undiplomatic?'

'Not that I noticed, Daphne,' he smiled. 'Sit down, girls, and I'll get you a drink of something – or would you prefer an ice?'

Gale swallowed and said,

'It's almost lunch time, Julius. Don't you think we ought to be moving?' Her challenging gaze informed him that she would subject his friend to some discomfort, should they stay, and Julius mildly agreed that it was rather late. But he again asked Daphne if he could fetch her anything from the little kiosk farther along the beach. She shook her head, her eyes fixed piercingly on Gale.

'No, thank you, Julius,' she murmured, and Gale allowed herself a most satisfied smile. Julius was the first to move; his action as he walked away surprised both girls, as it was so abrupt. Their eyes followed him as he slung the big towel over his shoulder. Daphne said, in tones soft and smooth as silk, 'You appear to have him just where you want him. How clever! Many women would be amazed, for docility is not a natural trait of the arrogant and masterful Julius Spiridon.' An invidious pause followed and then, 'You've obviously got something I haven't, for I could never have given him an order like that which you have just given him. But watch, my friend. Julius has never before been meek. . . .'

Smiling in a rather smug sort of way, Gale replied,

'Thanks for the warning – if that's what it's supposed to be. However, I don't need it. Goodbye; we'll meet again, seeing that we're neighbours.'

Julius had stopped, and he waited until Gale joined him. Her beach robe had been left at home, as had his, and she saw his eyes wander over her lovely figure. Lifting her face to give him an arch smile as she reached him, she instantly felt the smile freeze on her lips.

'Is anything wrong?' she asked, remembering what Daphne had just said about her giving Julius an order. 'You look vexed,' she added with well-simulated perplexity.

'Just you wait till I get you home,' he returned smoulderingly. 'You'll then find out what's wrong.'

A prickling sensation ran the length of Gale's spine. She suddenly wished she had her clothes on.

'I – I don't think I understand. Have I done something to annoy you?' Her voice was not quite steady, and certainly all her smug confidence had melted without trace. For the first time since she had met him she saw dark fury burning in his eyes, and the hand gripping the towel, a hand muscular and sensitive, was so tightly closed that the knuckle-bones seemed almost ready to break through the taut dark skin.

'Annoy!' Julius repeated, nostrils flaring. 'Do you really believe you can subject me to humiliation and get away with it?'

An unpleasant tightness settled in Gale's throat. She recalled that the only man ever to put fear into her was Julius, on that fatal morning when the burst pipe had been the instrument by which intended mischief was prevented. And now he was putting fear into her again; the knowledge created anger, but Gale prudently heeded the warning voice which was telling her to hold it in check. The wise way would be to apologize, she knew, but she found that impossible. In fact, she found it impossible to be meek, even.

'You're imagining things, Julius. Why should I want to subject you to humiliation?' The question seemed to set alight the smouldering embers of his wrath and she instantly regretted voicing it.

'You're going to learn, my girl, that it's fatal to give me an order—'

'Order?' she interrupted, striving now to dissipate his wrath because she was half afraid of going home with him in this mood. 'Oh, no, Julius!'

He was striding on towards where the car was parked at the rear of the beach; she trotted to keep up with him.

'I was left with the choice of humiliating you before Daphne – by putting you well and truly in your place – or agreeing to your order— *Order*!' he repeated grittingly, his added surge of fury manifested in his increased speed so that Gale had actually to skip a little now and then. 'Agreeing to your order that we go home,' he finished when at last he was able to speak.

Gale moistened her lips. Vaguely his words about putting her in her place registered. Why hadn't he – if he felt so strongly about the situation as he appeared to do? It would almost seem that he would suffer humiliation himself rather than have his wife put out of countenance before his ex-girl-friend. That Daphne had been his girl-friend was more than evident, proved by the words she had uttered about Gale's having something she had not, and also by the statement that Julius had never before been meek. Daphne knew him well, obviously.

'You're just exaggerating,' she began, but was instantly interrupted with,

'We're not having this out on the beach! I can hardly do what I want to do here!'

She swallowed moisture collecting on her tongue. The prickling sensation was there again; she felt really frightened now. What was he going to do to her?

'Wh-what are you threatening m-me with?' They had reached the car and Julius swung the door open with a savage gesture.

'Get in,' he commanded in a voice that now seemed to shake a little with the rage consuming him. Gale with a fleeting switch of memory recalled wishing several times lately that he would lose his temper, feeling it would be preferable to the cool austerity he sometimes adopted towards her when she was making herself particularly unpleasant. Well, here was her wish with a vengeance! This was in fact more than temper; it was white-hot fury. He stood beside her, waiting. So big he was, massive and towering! And Gale felt tiny in comparison. She knew an uncomfortable throbbing in her chest, and began to say she was not coming home with him, but his glance, sweeping over her scantily-clad figure, required no supplementing words to tell her of the sheer stupidity of that remark.

'Julius—' she began nervously, but before she could say more her arm was taken and she was roughly thrust into the front passenger seat of the car. The door slammed with unnecessary force and flinging the towel on to the back seat, Julius slid behind the wheel and within seconds the car shot forward, churning sand into a golden cloud behind it.

For a few awful moments there was silence in the car – more than silence, thought Gale, her heartbeats increasing as the distance between beach and home lessened, it was the hush of near-exploding wrath, the unearthly still before the storm. Her glance fell to her tiny covering, then rose to the profile of her husband and something akin to sheer terror assailed her.

'Julius,' she said huskily, having no idea what she meant to say next. He made no answer and she was left to find something, or again lapse into silence, which she could not because it was unbearable and too frightening and it set her imagination flowing to the scene which could be enacted once her husband had her in their room, at his mercy. 'If – if it s-sounded like an – an order,' she continued at length, saying what she hated saying but deciding that some effort must be made to appease him before they reached their villa, 'then I suppose I must apologize. I meant it only as a suggestion—'

Gale broke off for a moment, for his profile, so set and eagle-like, and the fingers on the car wheel, curling and uncurling in a way totally unlike their normal calm way of resting there, sent her nerves fluttering so uncomfortably that she actually felt short of breath. Those hands ... they looked as if they itched to strangle her! 'Yes, it was only meant as a suggestion,' she went on with a sort of breathless haste, noting they were already entering the long drive to the villa, 'because it w-was getting l-late.'

'You meant it as an order! – for Daphne's benefit! She'd riled you, and that was your method of retaliation!'

For a fleeting moment caution fled. Gale's hackles were well and truly up.

'If your girl-friends insult me then I shall most certainly retaliate. I told her she'd have to believe we were married simply because of what she had said previously. Perhaps I insulted her, but she started it—'

'I'm not talking about what you said to her,' he cut in raspingly. 'I'm talking about what you said to me, so don't try any evasion. Let me tell you, once and for all, that to adopt the high-handed manner with me will land you in a situation which will leave you smarting for a long while – as you're very soon going to discover.'

She went white, but contrived to say, repeating a

previous question,

'What exactly are you threatening me with, Julius?'

At that he actually stopped the car, took her chin in his hard hand and tilted her head up and round so roughly that something seemed to go taut in her neck.

'Any woman who thinks she can adopt that sort of attitude with me is in for trouble. You've been stepping close to the mark for a while, and this time you've been foolish enough to go over it. Perhaps I've misled you, having allowed you to get away with it up till now, portraying patience which I didn't feel. But nevertheless I have given you several warnings, hinted that you're playing a dangerous game, and had you known me better you'd have taken in the signs before now.'

Releasing her, he started the car again. 'You can prepare yourself for a most unpleasant few minutes,' he added, and once again caution went by the board as Gale said she hoped he wasn't threatening her with physical violence. At that he turned to glance at her and she heard him say, very softly now, but oh, with such deadly danger in his tones,

'If you're not careful you'll smart right now,' and, trembling visibly, Gale reached for the towel and put it over her legs. It was an automatic reaction, a compulsive act which she realized was rather silly. 'Do you suppose that will protect you?' he inquired in the same dangerously quiet tones.

She said nothing, merely tucking in the towel and then noticing they were already at the villa and Julius was bringing the car to a grinding halt before the front verandah. Was he intending to beat her? Opening her door with trembling fingers, she somehow managed to alight, even though her legs seemed almost to have lost their natural function of supporting her.

'Inside,' he ordered briefly, but although she managed to begin to obey him her footsteps flagged. With a roughly-taken grasp she was propelled towards the steps and helped in no uncertain manner up them. The towel was in her hand, trailing behind her, and Julius snatched it away and flung it over the rail.

'Julius,' she faltered, half turning to him, 'I'm – I'm very s-sorry. . . .' Her voice fell to silence; there was no mercy in those hard pagan features and those black-as-basalt eyes. Here was the type of Greek one read about – merciless when inspired by those heathen instincts inherited from ancestors who could torture and maim and kill without compunction.

'Your apology's come too late.' With a final shove he had her in the sitting-room. 'Upstairs,' he ordered. 'You've been asking for trouble since the day of our marriage, and now you're going to get it!'

CHAPTER SEVEN

WITH her heart beating over-rate, Gale backed away from her irate husband who, having closed the door behind him, stood against it, allowing his wrathful eyes to run over her before coming to rest on her colourless face. A degree of satisfaction entered their dark depths as she continued to lengthen the space between her husband and herself, coming to a halt only when the backs of her legs touched the bed.

'So you're afraid at last, are you?' The voice was quiet, but vibrating with fury that possessed him at the humiliation Gale had caused him. 'Come here,' he ordered, and pointed to a spot on the carpet which Gale looked at while remaining where she was.

'If you s-so m-much as lay a finger on me—' The words came to a choking halt as with three or four determined strides her husband reached her and she felt the force of his anger manifested in the ruthless grip of his hands on her bare arms.

'What are you threatening?' His face came close to hers; she could hear his sharpened breathing . . . a sign that his fury was still on the increase. 'Well? Answer me!'

She tried to swallow the ball of fear in her throat; Julius shook her and repeated his question.

'I don't know what your intention is, but—'

'Don't you!' Julius shook her with such violence that she felt her senses reeling and it did seem for one moment that she would completely lose consciousness, for even her mind was clouded over by her fear. If only he weren't so massive, and so strong, he might have made some attempt to free herself. 'So it hasn't entered your head that I might give you a damned good hiding?'

The colour rushed to her face, and even though the idea had occurred to her, out there in the car, which he had brought to such a violent halt, she flashed the threat at him that he had better not use violence, as she would go straight to the police. To her amazement he merely laughed harshly and reminded her that in Greece the husband was supreme master and if she was foolish enough to carry out her threat she would promptly be told to go back to her husband. She stared for a second in disbelief and then, her own anger rising above her fear, she endeavoured furiously to free herself from his vicious hold. It proved to be a futile attempt, and an exceedingly painful one, and she cried out in the end as, after his grip had tightened excruciatingly, he shook her again and again until at last the storm of his fury had abated.

'And now,' he said on releasing her, 'perhaps you'll think twice before allowing your tongue – and your temper – to run away with you again!'

The door closed, with unexpected quietness, the door between the two bedrooms. Gale stared at it, dazed still and bruised. Never had she visualized anyone being so inflamed as was Julius during that terrible few minutes through which she had passed. On entering the house she had known the instinct to call Kate, then restrained it, as it crossed her mind that the Greek servants were all inveterate gossipers, and the last thing Gale wanted was for Daphne to become possessed of the information that Gale's cleverness had brought down Julius's wrath upon her head.

'Be down for lunch in half an hour!' Julius's final order as he passed from her room into his still rang in

Gale's ears. She would *not* go down! She wasn't in a fit state to sit there, trying to assume a dignified manner, while Apollo and Kate waited on the table. Their eyes were keen, and Gale's face was swollen slightly, from the tears she had shed, and which fell now, the result of nervous reaction.

She washed and got dressed, then combed her hair. Julius was moving about in his room and she tapped lightly on his door.

'Come in.'

'I'm not feeling like lunch,' she told him without hesitation on seeing the slight inquiring lift of one eyebrow. Her eyes were still filmed with tears; all fight had been shaken out of her, but even now she was loath to let him see just how complete his victory had been, hence the rebellious glance she shot at him.

His basalt eyes narrowed to mere slits.

'Do you want some more?' he questioned softly.

She went red as fury rose, but dared not tempt him by defiance, for of a surety he would subject her to further discomfort should she not take care. Naturally making no answer, she backed into her room and quietly closed the door. Then the tears flowed freely once more. How had she got herself into a mess like this? Catching sight of her face in the mirror, she saw how white and drawn it was. Why had she married him . . .? Nothing to be gained by pretence regarding that. Yet hadn't she branded him ruthless and formidable, declaring that any woman who married him would require help from heaven? And after that she herself had married him, having fallen victim to his inescapable charm . . . his physical attraction that drew like a magnet, drew in such a way that even now she could not contemplate life without his lovemaking. Flushing with the shame of this admission, Gale went into the bathroom and bathed her eyes, trying the erase the evidence of her tears.

Julius was on the verandah when she entered the dining-room. He flicked a hand negligently, indicating a chair opposite the wicker couch on which he himself sat, and she made no hesitation but went through the french window and took the possession of the chair. She met his eyes as they lingered with faint mockery on her face, all his anger now dissolved, replaced by the more familiar languid manner of easy assurance and slight aloofness. Gale folded her hands together in her lap, determinedly concentrating on the lovely garden with its masses of exotic flowers whose perfume floated on to the verandah and would invade the dining-room, carried in by the *meltemi* – wind of the islands. Tangerine trees grew side by side with the delicately-flowered jacarandas; magnolias filled the air with their scent. Hibiscus of several colours grew among oleanders and other shrubs, and in glorious profusion the creepers scrambled over walls and invaded terraces, mingling with the trellised vines planted especially for shade. The passion flowers with their pinky blue and mauve stars were among the most beautiful of these climbers, but there was also the spiny bougainvillaea whose lovely red and orange and plummy purple flowers smothered large areas of the villa walls.

'So you decided it was more prudent to obey me,' observed Julius at last, and Gale turned her head, two spots of colour appearing in her cheeks at his use of the word obey. It was hardly necessary, but she guessed he enjoyed using it at this present time, after what had just happened, up there, in the bedroom. 'It's as well, Gale. Had you provoked me further I'd have given you something you would really remember.'

Something really to remember! Did he suppose she

would ever forget what he had done to her? On the contrary, it would be with her all her life, and Gale swore she would never forgive him for it. His gaze had moved from her to the garden and the olive slopes sweeping down to the beach beyond which the glimmering turquoise sea spread in lazy tranquillity towards the misted, dark rim of the horizon. Gale watched him in profile, and even now his attractiveness stimulated her senses in a way that thrilled while it angered. He was so very distinguished, with that aquiline nose, the finely-cut features, the aloof bearing and arrogance . . . and that iron-grey hair, which was thick and wavy, with its paler streaks resting against his brown temples.

Sensing her watchful eyes upon him, Julius turned his head and looked at her, disconcerting her by the sudden expression of satirical inquiry created by the widening of those incredibly dark eyes, and the slanting of an eyebrow. She tried to speak, but could find nothing to say. In any case, her husband's eyes were now moving from one bare arm to the other and . . . was it her imagination, or had that expression become slightly clouded? There certainly was no mistaking the frown line which appeared between his eyes. Deliberately she touched one tender bruise, fingering it lightly, and hoping the action would produce within him a feeling of self-blame. But instantly on noting his changing expression she admitted she had made a mistake. With keen perception he knew what she was about and a slight curve of his mouth portrayed amused contempt which was her sole reward for endeavouring to make him feel ashamed of himself.

'Just ring the bell, will you, Gale?' he commanded smoothly, flicking a languid hand to indicate the bell which was closer to her than to him. 'Apollo can serve the lunch now.'

Chastened, and with a spanked-child feeling, Gale obeyed, then rose from her chair. Julius rose also and reached for her hand as she would have passed him. And before she could collect herself at this unexpected action he was pressing his lips to hers in that masterful, possessive way which never failed to subdue any antagonism she might be feeling towards him. But his eyes glinted at the lack of response which on this particular occasion she was able to sustain.

'I should have beaten you,' he said decisively. 'It's the only way with a woman like you.' His arms were about her; momentarily his eyes moved to one of the bruises and he seemed to swallow something in his throat. But it was a fleeting gesture and one which, now that it was gone, left Gale in some doubt as to whether or not she had imagined it. 'Am I to take it that my kisses are not now welcome?' Despite the content of the question his air was one of supreme confidence. Drat the man! If only he would refrain from flaunting his superiority, his confidence of reducing her to complete surrender. Pompous, conceited creature, inflated by the arrogance of the conqueror! She said, tossing her head as she threw him a speaking glance,

'They're most *unwelcome*! I hate them!'

'How extraordinary,' he drawled, lazy suddenly and indifferent. 'I always had the impression that my kisses . . . and my caresses,' he added, slanting her an amused glance because already a blush had risen in advance of what he was about to say, 'gave you immense pleasure.'

She looked at him, her blush deepening.

'I once told you modesty was not one of your virtues,' she reminded him, acutely conscious of the touch of his hands on her arms even in this, one of her most alienated moods.

'And I said that insincerity was not one of my vices. You can't do without me, Gale, and yet you won't admit it—'

'I can do without you,' she flashed, twisting out of his grasp. 'I *can*!'

'Who are you trying to convince – yourself?' and he added before she could find a fitting retort to that, 'You're certainly not convincing me, my dear, and you never will. Come,' he said, suddenly brisk and impersonal, 'let's get our lunch. You'll feel better when you've eaten.'

She had known, all the afternoon and evening, that he would stay in his own room again tonight, and yet for a long while after getting into bed she had watched that door, slightly ajar, and shining brilliant white in the light from the moon streaming in through her window. She had watched it long and hard and in the end realizing she was almost willing it to move, move softly inwards, admitting her husband who would come to her, and look down from his superior height, look into her dreamy eyes for a long while before slipping out of his dressing-gown....

At last she slept, fitfully as on the previous night. And she awoke tired and unhappy and with an almost irrepressible inclination to go into her husband's room and talk. About what? How did a wife go to her husband and inform him that she wanted him? A deep sigh escaped her. There was still the world of differences between the privileges of the sexes. Julius could come to her, but she could not go to him— She could, of course, but what sort of a reception would she get? If Julius had wanted her he would have come.... Or was he deliberately testing her? He'd firmly asserted that she couldn't do without him, had confidently declared that his kisses and caresses gave her immense pleasure.

And of course he was right.

So now he was testing her. Suddenly she had no doubts at all about the reason for his staying away from her. Her blood boiled. He would be the one to regret this! For when he did come, which he would – oh, yes, Gale was very sure of that – when he did come, then she would show him whether she could do without him or not! Whatever the effort she would resist him. He should not continue in this state of arrogant confidence that he had married a woman whom he could without effort reduce to his willing and eager slave. She was no Greek girl – servile because she had been brought up to regard the male sex as superior in every sense of the word. If that was what Julius wanted then he should have married one of his own kind.

After bathing and dressing Gale listened automatically for his outer door to open, and for him to go downstairs, but all was silent. Surely he wasn't still sleeping? With a shrug she went down. He was already at the breakfast table and had actually started eating. She stood in the doorway for a long moment, staring in disbelief. Julius, a stickler for etiquette, had never before begun a meal until she herself had put in an appearance.

'Have you been down long?' The question was put as she sat down, the product of awkwardness. She never even looked at him as, picking up a spoon, she dug it into the grapefruit Apollo had placed ready for her.

'Twenty minutes or so.' A pause and then, 'Sleep well?'

She licked her lips.

'Of course. Did you?'

He laughed and shook his head, not in a negative gesture but in one of impatience amounting almost to asperity.

'I happen to be one of those fortunate people who rarely finds sleep elusive. Yes, my dear Gale, I slept like a log, thank you.'

He was laughing at her, inwardly. On the surface his manner became indifferent, and the meal was eaten without further words passing between him and his wife.

And this state of indifference on his part and of stubbornness on Gale's continued for the next three days. They swam each morning, but were almost as strangers. Daphne joined them on one occasion and the difference in Julius's manner was quite literally staggering. He smiled and chatted; he laughed at his ex-girl-friend's jokes, and finally asked her up to the villa for lunch the following day.

'I'm not having her at my table!' snapped Gale as they drove home. 'I can't think how you could ask her. It's a disgraceful thing to harbour one of your – your—' She broke off on noting the sudden compression of her husband's mouth. A repetition of that other scene was the last thing she desired, so she prudently re-phrased her words. 'It isn't very nice of you to bring Daphne to our house. You know full well it will embarrass me.'

'Just a neighbourly gesture,' he returned without the slightest interest. 'She'll probably ask us up to her place very shortly.'

'I shan't go!'

'That's up to you. I shall most certainly accept her invitation.'

'I'm not having her tomorrow,' Gale warned again, and this time her husband's head shot round and she noted the glint in his eye and the flaring of his nostrils, as on that other occasion.

'You have no say in the matter,' he told her crisply. 'Watch yourself, Gale, you've already had a demonstration of my temper. I should have thought it would be the last thing you'd want to see again.'

'You're threatening me with violence if I refuse to have Daphne in our home?'

'I've just said you've no say in the matter,' he reminded her. 'Daphne comes to lunch tomorrow and you will be civil to her. Understand?'

'I can't be civil to her!' To her own amazement tears came readily to her eyes. 'I hate her! So how can I be civil to her?'

'Hate her, do you ...?' almost to himself as he brought the car on to the front by the verandah. 'That's rather a strong word, surely?'

'Dislike, then. I shan't be at all comfortable sitting at the same table as one of the women you've had in the past.'

Amused at her way of putting it, Julius slanted her a humorous glance as he slid from the car and came round to her side.

'One of them?' His hand was oddly gentle on her arm as he helped her from the car. This gentleness hurt, somehow, in a way she could not fathom. His touch was gentle when he made love to her, but this was the first time he had shown gentleness on any other occasion.

'You admitted you'd had lots of women,' Gale reminded him, and he nodded, as if admitting it again, now that she had refreshed his memory. 'It's – different when a wife doesn't know them,' she went on, although she could not have given a reason for this trend of thought which she was allowing her husband to share. 'She isn't troubled—'

'Troubled?' He was close, and his hand touched her chin, tilting it so that he could read what was written in her eyes. She lowered her lashes, and again she found no reason for what she did. Somehow, though, it seemed imperative that he should not subject her to one of his searching, penetrating looks. 'Are my past amours liable to trouble you, Gale?' His fingers moved idly over her arm and as always she was profoundly aware of the pleasure of his touch. She glanced down as a movement at her feet caught her attention momentarily. A pretty pink and green lizard was darting about on the paving stones. 'I've asked you a question,' her husband reminded her gently, and she looked up then, aware that her eyes were clouded slightly.

'Don't misunderstand me,' she began, wondering why she wasn't flashing out the words at him, as would have been more appropriate to a situation such as this, when her husband's past was being discussed. 'It's only Daphne – and that's because I've met her.' She paused, expecting some comment, but Julius was merely staring down at her and waiting patiently for her to continue. 'How would you like it if I invited one of my ex-boy-friends to the house?'

The silence continued, but all at once her husband's expression changed. He looked like a fiend, she thought, shuddering automatically as the scene of a few days ago returned with frightening force. The gentle touch on her arm became a vice of pain and she cried out, wondering vaguely if she were to carry his bruises permanently, since she had not yet got rid of the others and now she was sure he had inflicted more.

'I'm sorry, Gale,' he said, surprisingly. 'I didn't mean to hurt you.'

She said, because some compulsive force directed her, almost against her will,

'You haven't answered my question, Julius.'

Glinting eyes and a stern set to his mouth. A muscle out of control in his jaw, but arrogance and mastery in the voice he used, as, patting her cheek as he had done once before, he said,

'I should probably strangle you, my dear.'

She gaped, and remained fixed to the spot even though Julius made to move away.

'And yet you expect me to have Daphne here?'

'Men are privileged to keep up old friendships. Women are expected to be more circumspect.' So bland the words. Gale could have believed he was teasing her if it hadn't been for his expression, which clearly told her that he most certainly was not.

'I shan't be civil to her,' Gale was saying again the following day just before their guest was expected. 'In fact, I've a good mind to leave you both alone.'

He shrugged his shoulders.

'If you prefer to lunch alone, then by all means do so,' he said, staggering her.

'Tell me,' she inquired suddenly, 'what exactly are you trying to do to me?'

A cool inquiring glance came her way, and she heard an odd inflection in her husband's voice when he spoke, saying he did not quite understand.

'You'll have to be more explicit,' he added, his eyes fixed with keen interest on her face.

'You're not the same?'

'In what way not the same?'

She hesitated, her brow puckering as words became difficult to voice.

'Well . . . lately . . .' But she tailed off, soft colour rising owing to her thoughts, and because of the fact that Julius was under no illusions about these thoughts.

'Yes, my dear,' he prompted gently, 'you were about

to say something?'

She swallowed hard.

'You should know in what way you've changed.' Why speak like this? she asked herself. She ought to be telling him outright that he was playing a game with her. Why couldn't she say she didn't care if he kept to his own room? – inform him airily that it could go on like this? How was it that the resolve she had made was not presented openly to him – the resolve that their relationship should continue as it was at present, seeing that it was Julius himself who had started it all?

'Can it be,' he murmured with infuriating calm not untinged with humour, 'that you are missing my kisses ... and caresses, despite your attitude to the contrary?'

'Certainly not! That wasn't what I meant at all!' Would he know she lied? It was more than likely, Gale owned, for Julius was more than ordinarily astute.

'No?' He stifled a yawn and glanced at his watch. 'Daphne should be on her way by now; I'll go and meet her as she's bound to be walking. You can look over the table, and see that Kate has it just as it should be. Oh, and if you have decided to lunch alone, then make sure your place is cleared.'

She glared at him as he went off, through the french window on to the patio and took the steps in a couple of light athletic leaps.

'I hate you!' she whispered fiercely to his disappearing broad straight back. 'I wish with all my heart I'd never married you!'

She did not lunch alone, as she had known from the first she wouldn't. Why should she leave them together – to chat over old times? If they desired to do that then they could make some other arrangements. Gale checked thoughts like these, suddenly admitting that she would be plunged into the depths of misery if her husband and Daphne were to begin seeing each other again. It never dawned on her to question this new emotion which was drawing her into its net. Not for one moment would she have entertained the idea that she was jealous of the other girl.

Daphne looked ravishing in a strapless cotton dress trimmed with embroidery at the waist and hem. She wore a jewelled bracelet and earrings to match, and something in the way she kept on flicking the bracelet before Julius's eyes convinced Gale that the beautiful, expensive set had at one time been a gift from him . . . for favours received? The idea hurt and a sudden frown lightly touched Gale's wide brow. At that moment Julius caught her expression and he lifted an eyebrow in an interrogating gesture. She looked away, and became absorbed in her own thoughts. Daphne was chattering, talking about parties and various other functions which she had recently attended Julius put in a word now and then, and this appeared to provide all the encouragement the girl required for the eager continuance of her inane chatter.

'You miss half the social activities, Julius,' Daphne was saying. 'Aren't you interested, now that you're married?'

'I've never been interested to the same extent as you, Daphne.'

The girl was probably bored half her time, concluded Gale spitefully – but then wondered how she herself would feel when her own time came, and Julius was lost to her for ever – as one day he must be lost, there being no solid foundation to their marriage. Based on nothing more substantial than physical desire, it must inevitably topple and become as unreal as a dream.

Gale felt choked, suddenly, and her knife and fork was put on to her plate with a little clatter. Was anything wrong? her husband's inquiring glance said, and she picked up her fork again and toyed with the meat on her plate. What was this unfamiliar pang which passed through her at the idea of losing Julius? Gale would have analysed it, or attempted to, but Daphne was speaking, describing the yacht her father had recently bought and which was moored just off the shore at the sandy bay of Griko. Julius was intensely interested, nodding now and then as if approving the features which were being enlarged upon by their guest.

'Father's giving a party aboard shortly,' Daphne went on, using those long mascaraed lashes to the best effect she knew. 'You'll come, of course?'

'If we're invited; yes, most certainly we shall come.'

Daphne replied to the effect that of course they would be invited, and as Julius then spoke in his turn Gale allowed their conversation to drift on, uninterrupted by any participation from her. One or twice Julius would glance at her as if inviting her to take part, but curiously enough she was content to listen – or vaguely listen, as her main trend of thought was still on the eventuality of the parting.

She herself had initially owned that their ardour must wane and had surmised that she would have been just as ready for the separation as her husband. Permanent marriage had been anticipated once in her life – when she became engaged to Michael, but since the age of eighteen it had held no attraction for her. To be in love was disastrous, she had long since decided. One left oneself open to the wounds which men in their inherent ruthlessness could inflict over and over again.

This risk was not one which Gale was willing to take a second time. With Julius, the one and only emotion had been the desire for him to make love to her.

She admitted without restraint that what she felt on that morning at the lodge was a deep and aching disappointment. Subconsciously she had cursed the intervention of fate which had, as Julius had put it, 'saved' her. Reflectively she wondered what would have been the ultimate result of her surrender. Not marriage, that was for sure. Greeks never married the women they seduced. No, it would have been an affair, since Gale now fully owned that Julius was right when he suggested she would feel differently afterwards.

An affair ... How long would it have been before Julius had tired of her? Until some other woman came along. ... This trend naturally brought her attention to the lovely girl seated at their luncheon table. Julius had obviously tired of her ... and yet they were friends still. A frown crossed Gale's forehead. When this happened to her, she would never go near Julius again – and most certainly she could not bear to be in the company of the woman whose charms had been so appealing to Julius that she had supplanted her.

Julius was suggesting they take coffee on the patio and they all rose from the table. His hand went to Daphne's elbow. Gale's teeth snapped together. What need was there for the girl to be assisted over the threshold of the dining-room on to the patio outside? But Daphne liked it, obviously, because she covered Julius's hand with hers as if she would prevent him from removing it.

'Gale dear, take the other chair; then you can have the coffee tray on that small table over there.'

She glared at him, because he had afforded *her* no attention at all. Raising his brows in a gesture of inquiry, he served only to produce another glowering look and, shrugging languidly, he extended his wife no further interest at all, and when the time came for Daphne to leave he accompanied her home.

Watching them from the patio as they wandered along the tree-shaded drive towards the road, Gale felt something far deeper than anger rise within her. It was a strange and incomprehensible feeling, rather like a dead weight, yet sort of empty too. What was it? – this so new and troublesome thing that had taken possession of her? Pensively she kept her eyes on the pair until they reached the curve where they stopped a moment, to speak, and a dark frown marred the beauty of Gale's face. Why stop? They could carry on a conversation while walking. Gale's eyes narrowed as, after a backward glance so fleeting that it was scarcely noticeable, Julius slipped a hand beneath his companion's arm and they walked on again, to become lost to sight round the bend.

Gale moistened her lips. That earlier pang was felt again, and this time it hurt so deeply that she knew she must probe the reason for it. Did she need to probe very far? The pang was born of fear, she told herself – fear that her husband would be unfaithful to her, would decide his former lover was, after all, more desirable than his wife.

CHAPTER EIGHT

On his return Julius gave his wife the dismaying news that he was going to Munich on business and would be away about a fortnight.

'So long?' she quivered. 'Can't I come with you?'

He shook his head, telling her that as he would be engaged all the time on business matters she would find it dull.

'I'd not even be able to spend the evenings with you, as we frequently discuss business over a dinner. You can explore the island,' he suggested without much interest. 'We've done a little, but not all by any means, Get Apollo to drive you to some of the interesting places.'

He set off early the following morning, Apollo driving him to the port where he would board a ferry which would take him to Rhodes, from he would make air connections.

A fortnight. . . . It seemed a long time, Gale thought, but then she recalled that he had once or twice spent that length of time in England. What should she do with her time? She could have gone to England. She still could! Yes, she would go home for ten days or so.

Apollo helped in every way, having knowledge of the aeroplanes from Rhodes and their times of departure. Kate packed for her and only two days after her husband had left for Munich Gale was on her way to England, having sent her mother a cable letting her know the approximate time of arrival. But to her surprise there was no one in when she reached home and she had to while way a couple of hours until her father put in an appearance at half-past five.

'Your mother's on holiday,' he snapped even before his key was in the lock. 'I got your cable, but I had commitments at the university and couldn't be here when you arrived.'

'Mother's on holiday?' Gale half-turned as she stepped into the hall, preceding her father. 'She never goes on holiday!'

He seemed to grit his teeth – Gale could not be sure of this, but she was sure of the slamming of the door. The whole house shuddered!

'Your mother does a lot of things lately she's never done before!' He swept an illustrative gesture around the sitting-room as they entered it. 'Damned place hasn't seen a duster since she went! I've not had a decent meal, either!'

'Where's she gone?' Gale put down her suitcase and shook her head disbelievingly. 'When did she go?'

'She went a week today! And she's gone to Cornwall!' He flung his briefcase on to the couch and glared at his daughter. 'Can't say I'm overjoyed to see you at this time,' he growled, going on to declare that it was all her fault for carrying on the way she had. 'If you must have a good time in that way then why the devil didn't you do it on the sly!'

Angry colour fused her cheeks. Already she regretted the hasty decision that had resulted in her coming home.

'Do you do it on the sly?' she had to ask, sending him a glance of contempt.

'Shut up about my affairs! What's wrong with you anyway? Your marriage cracked up already?'

Her colour heightened.

'Julius is away on business; that's why I'm here. I thought it would be nice to see Mother – and you,' she added as an afterthought, bringing a sneer to her father's lips.

'You wouldn't care if you never saw me again, so don't give me that rubbish!' He paced about for a few wrathful seconds before coming to a halt close to where Gale stood, still in her outdoor things. 'You've ruined both our lives; I hope you're proud of yourself!'

'Don't shift the blame, Father. You and Mother have had nothing between you for a long while – but why should you need reminding of this? You know who's to blame if things are not what they were.'

'She was resigned! It was only when you let her down that she turned. I still can't believe it!'

Slowly Gale unbuttoned the jacket of her suit and took it off.

'You have Mother's address?'

'I have not! Refused to give it. I swore I'd not allow her to go off on her own – on her own,' he said in snarling accents. 'Do you suppose she's with a man?'

'Certainly not!' But Gale was not sure. It would appear that her mother had gone on holiday with Jack, incredible as it seemed. 'You were saying you wouldn't let her go away . . .?'

'Yes, I told her straight she wasn't going and that was that. She made no argument and I thought that was the end of it. I came home from work a couple of days later to find a note. She'd gone off to Cornwall for a fortnight! My God, I wouldn't have given her as much housekeeping money if I'd known she could save for a fortnight's holiday!' He looked Gale over, diverted for a space as he noted the very expensive outfit she wore and the soft leather suitcase beside her, with her monogram embossed in gold on the lid. 'Did well for yourself – after all that rot you used to talk about never getting married—' Breaking off, he wagged a forefinger at her. 'Something fishy about that affair, too. Damned odd that he'd marry you if he could get you without—'

'Stop it! He did not – not – get me without, as you so vulgarly term it.'

He shrugged . . . and suddenly she noticed a faint heaviness in his breathing which caused an involuntary catch of her own breath. It could be the result of temper, of course, but. . . . Suddenly Gale did not like the look of him.

'Are you going to get me some tea, seeing that you're here?' he demanded.

Gale nodded but hesitated, dropping her jacket over the back of a chair.

'Are you feeling all right? I mean – you're not off-colour?'

He glowered at her and thumbed towards the door.

'I'm fit enough! It's my mind that's troubled. Get me something to eat. You know where the kitchen is!'

'Are you going out this evening?' she was inquiring later as they sat together eating the meal she had prepared from what little she could find in the fridge.

'I am! And have you anything to say about it?' he added challengingly, his whole manner one of belligerence.

'Nothing at all,' returned Gale calmly. 'I merely asked because I've no intention of sitting here on my own.'

'So you're going out too? Seeing one of your boyfriends?'

She ignored that – she had to, otherwise there would have been one big row and she'd have found herself on the plane again, returning to Greece. She wanted to see her mother, who would be back in a week's time. They would have three days together, Gale hoped. But if she quarrelled with her father in the meantime she could scarcely remain at home.

'Don't wait up for me,' her father said as he went out after washing and changing and fixing a carnation in his buttonhole. 'I'll be late.'

So that was that. Gale looked at the closed door of the sitting-room and breathed a deep sigh. What a homecoming! No welcome from either of her parents. Just an empty house with an atmosphere of disunity seeming to pervade every corner of it. She glanced around, automatically comparing the room with that in which she and Julius sat when they were not out on the verandah or in the dining-room. Again she heaved a sigh. Her mother had tried so hard, but there was so little on which to indulge her artistic instincts. It had been a hard life, and a not very happy one. No luxuries simply because her husband squandered the greater part of his salary on other women. This naturally brought Gale's thoughts back to this holiday of her mother's. Had she saved for it or had her man friend paid for it? Baffled and unable to envisage her mother going off on holiday with another man, Gale shook her head from side to side. It was not feasible, she told herself – and yet who else was there with whom her mother could go away? As far as Gale knew she had never made a woman friend, and she had no sisters or cousins.

'It's a mystery,' she sighed, rising and going to the

door. 'And if Mother was going away, she might have mentioned it in one of her letters.'

Gale went up to the old room she had occupied when at home. She had told her father she had no intention of sitting in the house all evening on her own, but where could she go? There was Tricia, of course, and one or two other of her old friends. . . . Suddenly Gale felt lost and alone – utterly alone. The reason was that she had looked forward eagerly to seeing her mother, to chatting with her as they used to do in the days before the incident at the lodge had brought such disunity into the house. Gale believed that her marriage to Julius had put right the position between her and her mother and indeed her mother's letters had all been affectionate, and each had included the hope that Gale was happy with her husband.

And yet no mention of this holiday had ever been made.

Endeavouring to thrust from her the disappointment at not finding her mother at home, Gale washed and changed and applied a little make-up to her cheeks and lips. Then she went out, called a taxi and after stopping at a telephone box to discover if Tricia was at home, she directed the driver to take her to the Sims' house where she was greeted enthusiastically by Mrs. Sims and her daughter, both of whom were in the garden, relaxing in chairs on the lawn.

'How very nice to see you, Gale dear! We had no idea you were in England until you phoned. Sit down and tell us why you're here and how long you're staying. It's Tricia's twenty-first birthday on Monday. Will you have left by then? We're giving a party for her.'

Her spirits lightening at this reception, Gale smiled and took the chair offered.

'No, I'll still be here. I'd love to come to the party.' She went on to explain how she came to be here without her husband. Her eyes strayed several times to Tricia's face and she saw by her shadowed expression that she had not yet recovered from the loss of her fiancé to another girl. Nevertheless, she was far more composed than when on that fatal day she had suggested Gale should attempt to bring Trevis to disgrace in the eyes of the man whose daughter he hoped to marry.

'She's met someone else,' Mrs. Sims told Gale when for a few minutes they were alone in the living-room while Tricia was upstairs tidying herself up before supper. 'But although both her father and I like him enormously Tricia is merely lukewarm about the whole affair. I do believe she would forgive Trevis even now if he should turn up and ask her to take him back.'

It was clear that Tricia had not enlightened her mother about the affair at the lodge. Gale said, frowning a little,

'It takes a long while to get over being jilted. There's the pride element in addition to the heartache. A girl gets an outsize inferiority complex when the man whom she loves, and who has chosen her as his wife, suddenly discovers he prefers someone else.'

Mrs. Sims nodded understandingly.

'I realize that, Gale. And of course Tricia is the type who has little confidence in her own attractions anyway. And with Stephen – that's the boy she goes out with now and then – she's convinced that if she lets herself fall in love with him he'll treat her as Trevis did. It's no use trying to persuade her that this isn't so; she won't listen either to her father or to me.'

Gale nodded.

'I felt like that,' she reminded her friend's mother.

'For a long time – yes, indeed. But you're happily married now. How surprised we all were! Gale of all people, I said to my husband. Gale, who always swore she'd never marry. But your Julius is inordinately handsome, I'm told?'

'He is, yes.' Gale felt shy – a rather new experience for her – and she lowered her head, faintly embarrassed by Mrs. Sims' amused gaze.

'Tell me about your house,' urged Mrs. Sims, whose interest was plainly genuine. 'Your husband's a very wealthy man, so the rumour goes, and I expect it's true, even though rumours are more often false.'

'It's a beautiful house, with pretty gardens and magnificent views over the lower part of the hills and the beach, to the sea.'

'You're a very lucky girl,' returned Mrs. Sims, and added, her voice adopting a note of anxiety, 'I do wish Tricia were settled.'

'She will be,' Gale asserted with confidence. 'This Stephen – would he like to be serious with her?'

'He's confided in me that he would.'

'Does he know about Trevis?'

Mrs. Sims nodded her head.

'Yes, he knows. He says Trevis was a fool to lose her.'

A faintly bitter curve touched Gale's full wide mouth.

'That isn't much consolation to Tricia.'

'I suppose people said something of the kind to you?'

'They did, but it wasn't any help.' She paused a moment, reflectively. 'It's rather strange, now, to think how deeply affected I was at the time. You think you'll never get over these things, but you do.'

'It's like having a death in the family. When I lost my first husband I thought I'd die. And yet the time came when I found to my surprise that I could love again – as you have done, Gale. I've tried to convince Tricia that it's possible to love more than once, but when one is young one finds this difficult to believe.'

Gale was strangely silent, impressed by her companion's words in some way she could not at present define. The only surface emotion she experienced was one of guilt – she felt a hypocrite for allowing Mrs. Sims to believe she was in love with Julius. It was rather like living a lie.

During supper, at which Mr. Sims was also present, Tricia suggested that, as Mrs. Davis was not at home, Gale should spend a few days with her friend.

'That is,' Tricia added, 'if your father wouldn't mind.'

'I don't expect he would,' responded Gale, hoping the dry note in her voice had escaped everyone's ears.

'You'll come, then?'

'Yes – and thank you for asking me. When shall I come?'

'This week-end – or any time to suit you.' Mrs. Sims looked questioningly at her. 'I expect you've other friends to visit while you're over?'

'Just one or two,' replied Gale absently, reflecting on how quickly one lost touch after marriage. Letters had been sent and received from one or two of the crowd Gale used to go about with, but a lack of enthusiasm was gradually creeping in.

It was arranged that Gale should go to the Sims on the Friday morning and stay until about Monday or

Tuesday, depending on how she felt. The party was to be at the Roebuck Hotel in Burton and Gale had the pleasure of buying herself a new dress for the occasion, not having brought anything at all formal with her. She also shopped around for a suitable present for Tricia, and also one for Mrs. Sims, just as a token of thanks for having her.

Much to her surprise Gale met with some slight opposition from her father when she told him of the invitation, which, she added, she had accepted.

'You're going off and leaving me on my own? That's a fine thing! If you think anything of your father you'll turn down the invitation – which should never have been made, seeing as you're here only for a short time.'

'I didn't expect you'd care what I did. You intend to stay in at night with me – if I decide to turn down the invitation?' she queried, having not the least intention of giving back word to Mrs. Sims.

'Stay in?' He raised his brows. 'I never stay in.'

'Then you'll not miss me,' she pointed out suavely.

'Breakfast and tea,' he snapped. 'I'd like a decent meal or two put before me.'

Her eyes raked him with contempt.

'I'm not Mother,' she told him softly.

'None of your damned cheek, Gale! You used to know how to respect your father. Are you turning down that invitation or aren't you?'

'I'm not. What would I do here all day by myself? And what sort of evening would I spend, sitting here alone?'

'You could get busy with some housework—'

'Housework?' she interrupted, staring at him in a way which could only be described as one of hauteur. 'I haven't come all this way to spend my time in housework. I'm on holiday.'

'Too high-and-mighty, eh – now that you've managed to land yourself a rich husband?'

'If Mother were at home I should naturally help her, as I always did, but as she isn't home I'm going to stay with Tricia and her people.'

'The place hasn't been touched for a week!'

'I don't suppose you notice any difference. I've never once heard you comment no matter how hard Mother's worked to make the place look nice.'

He said nothing to that, but went out and left her to her own devices. She washed the dishes and then went by taxi to see another friend. But she didn't stay long and she was in bed by half-past nine.

She lay there, thinking of Julius and wondering what he was doing. He'd be enjoying himself, no mistake about that. These business trips which men took were invariably pleasure trips as well, Gale thought, recalling how her husband used to attend all the parties when he was in England. Perhaps he had some friend in Munich, some friend like Professor Ingham who would introduce him into a circle similar to that to which his friend had introduced him here.

'He could have taken me with him,' she said in muffled tones, her face in the pillow. 'I'm sure he could – if he'd wanted to.'

Obviously he had not wanted to.

In spite of what she had said Gale spent the whole of Thursday cleaning the house. She cooked a tasty meal for when her father returned in the late afternoon. He neither commented on the meal nor noticed what she had done in the house, even though she had put clean pyjamas on his bed and washed and ironed all his shirts and other clothes which she found in the linen basket.

'I'll see you some time, then,' he said on the Friday morning as he went out. 'Enjoy yourself,' he added peevishly – like a spoiled child, she thought. 'And don't let your conscience prick you!'

'I won't,' she shot back, but in a voice of sweetness which was rewarded with a glowering look.

'You're your mother's daughter – no mistake about that,' he snarled, and went out, slamming the door behind him.

She washed the breakfast dishes, set the table for his tea, made his bed, and generally left everything tidy before leaving home. It afforded her satisfaction even though she knew very well that he would no more notice what she had done today than he had noticed last evening.

Tricia's party was in effect a dinner-dance. Gale met Stephen and liked him enormously. They danced together and later she told Tricia that she considered her most fortunate in having Stephen for a friend. On seeing Tricia's eyes light up as they sought the figure of Stephen among a group of young men, Gale said no more. Tricia was getting over Trevis – slowly perhaps, but quite surely for all that.

On dancing with Dave Ingham later Gale was asked about her husband.

'He's in Munich,' she told him, 'on business.'

'And so you decided to come home and see your friends?'

'I came primarily to see Mother, but unfortunately for me she's on holiday. That's why I'm staying with Tricia.' Professor Ingham made no comment and after a while she said hesitantly, 'Do you ever see Trevis?'

'On occasions,' he replied guardedly.

There was another long hesitation before Gale said, 'Does he still go up to the lodge?'

'I believe he does.' The non-committal reply should by rights have deterred her from further mention of the subject, but she seemed to be under the effect of some irrepressible force and she asked him if friends still used the lodge when Trevis was not there himself. She glanced up into her partner's face as she spoke and surprised a strange smile lifting the corners of his mouth. For some incomprehensible reason she was taken in memory back to that night when she had overheard the conversation of this man and Julius, the conversation that made her blood boil at the derogatory manner in which her sex was discussed.

'Trevis does let friends have his lodge, yes.'

Gale took an impatient breath because her subtle inquiries brought no information whatsoever, and she remained silent, following her partner's steps and giving herself up to the pleasure of the dance, even though her mind was on her husband, and the way he danced, so superbly and with the arrogant grace of the ancient Hellenic athletes. 'You've gone very quiet,' observed her partner after a while, in what could only be described as tones of amusement.

'Your answers to my questions are so brief and unrevealing that talking seems to be a waste of time,' she told him frankly, and to her surprise he laughed.

'You mean, questions are a waste of time, don't you?'

She went red.

'Shall we change the subject, Dave?'

'No, I don't think we will. What is it that you want to know?'

She had to laugh then, and said,

'Tell me, do you happen to know how Julius and I came to get married?' Gale regretted the question the moment it was uttered, despite the fact that she had been asking it, in a most roundabout way, for the past few minutes or so. It seemed too intimate now that it was put into plain words; it was not a thing to be brought out like this, even though Dave was her husband's friend, his trusted friend, of long standing.

'You're asking if Julius has confided something to me?'

She did not answer immediately, but endeavoured to read his expression first. There was nothing to infer from it except the faintest hint of puzzlement. This was all she required, though, to answer her question.

'Obviously he didn't confide anything in you,' she stated, and when he shook his head briefly she added, 'Forget it, please.'

He frowned at her.

'You have me puzzled, Gale. Was your marriage not as ordinary a business as it appeared? I must admit we were all rather surprised at Julius—' He stopped, then grinned and carried on, but in tones of faint apology. 'He was considered to be the confirmed bachelor and so naturally his marriage caused a stir. It was all done so quietly too, and so hurriedly. But I myself knew he was attracted to you, so the idea that there was something not quite straightforward about the marriage never entered my head. Now, however, you have me thinking – and puzzled. Want to confide?'

She bit her lip, angry with herself for her persistence in putting the question which had resulted in arousing his curiosity, and putting thoughts into his head that had not been there before.

'No, I don't want to confide,' she answered firmly, then added, 'How did you know he was – was attracted to me?'

Professor Ingham shrugged his shoulders.

'It was obvious. He was always looking at you – I think many of us knew how he was feeling about you.'

Gale reflected on these words, recalling her brother's declaring that Julius was affected by her beauty, that he hadn't taken his eyes off her the whole evening. Where Dave had made the mistake was that he had concluded that his friend's interest was love . . . or had he? Some catch of nerves set her alert to the possibility that Dave was under no illusions as to the nature of the attraction which Julius had found in her. The idea made her go hot all over, more especially as she was once again hearing that discussion between Julius and Dave out in the garden on the evening of the barbecue. They had been laughing, talking in such contemptuous terms about women. So completely without strength of character, Dave had said. And they were so very easy to conquer. Julius had agreed, but added that he preferred a fight. And it was then he had gone on to say the thing that set the blood pounding in Gale's head, so heightened had been her temper. 'Place your hand on a woman's heart and she's yours instantly.'

The music stopped and it was with relief that Gale found herself being led from the floor back to the table. She was filllled with a sense of embarrassment, and of shame. It was unbearable to dwell on the idea that Dave – and probably everyone else – believed the tall handsome Greek, who had been regarded as a confirmed bachelor, had married Gale simply for desire. And yet Gale did dwell on it because she could not dismiss it from her mind. The evening was spoilt by it, for she fairly squirmed inside. And now and then she would glance around, watching faces and expressions whenever anyone happened to look her way. What were they thinking? she asked herself, and she would have to lower her head, sure that her colour had risen.

Towards the end of the evening she sat with Tricia, under a potted palm tree in the corner of the room, and they chatted as they sipped their drinks. But Gale was fated once again to overhear Professor Ingham, and this time he was talking to someone whose voice Gale did not recognize, but Tricia told her later that he was a friend of her father and his name was Lawrence Hyatt. The two men were sitting on the other side of a nearby alcove and the girls had no idea they were so close until Dave's voice was heard.

'You saw him in Paris? Are you sure? He told his wife he was going to Munich.'

'Of course I'm sure. I know him well by sight – I was at the barbecue, remember. He was with a blonde.'

'He's only been married a few weeks. Was the girl English?'

'Very English.'

'Julius with a blonde in Paris! Well, well . . .!'

Both girls had been speechless up to this point, but now both spoke at once, Tricia saying,

'Let's get away from here—' and Gale, white to the lips, managing a very unsteady,

'Shall we . . . move?'

'Gale,' began Tricia when they were some distance away from where they had been sitting, 'take no notice. It isn't true. You know what men are when they get talking . . .!' Her voice trailed off as she became aware of how futile her efforts at comfort were.

'Of course it's true.' Gale's voice was scarcely audible. She felt almost physically ill and would have given anything to be transported into her own room at home, where she could hide away and not let anyone see this cloak of sheer misery that had wrapped itself around her on hearing those words uttered.

Julius in Paris – the gay city of story and song. Julius in Paris . . . with a blonde. Was the blonde's name Daphne? Or was her husband with some other girl?

Gale thought of her father and of Malcolm and Trevis – and she hated all men! Yes, all of them.

'None of them are any good,' she quivered, talking to herself. Tears fought for release, but Gale remembered all at once that this was her friend's party and she made a supreme effort to hold them back, succeeding only after she had rubbed her eyes hard so that the moisture had been pressed on to her fingers.

'I'm so sorry.' Tricia herself seemed almost distracted. 'I don't know what to say.'

'There's nothing to say. Let's forget it! Shall we have another drink?'

'I'm sure there must be some mistake,' persisted Tricia. 'Why can't we go and speak to those two and find out what that friend of Father's really meant?'

'There's been no mistake. As for speaking to them—' Gale swallowed hard. 'That's the last thing I'd do.' She looked mistily at her friend. 'You know the circumstances of our marriage, so it's no use my pretending that Julius is in love with me.'

Tricia stared in bewilderment.

'Then why did he marry you? Oh, I know all about your mother, and the way she felt – you told me all that at the time. But Julius had no need to marry you.

There must have been some attraction. Besides, everybody used to notice how he looked at you. And I do know that at one party he told Professor Ingham that there was only one attractive girl in the whole place, and it was you. Yes, there was some good reason for his marrying you, no matter what you say about his not being in love with you.' Tricia believed she was helping, and only realized her mistake when Gale, feeling there was no need for the least secrecy or restraint now – after what Tricia had overheard – told her that the only appeal she had for Julius was that of desire.

'Greeks are notorious for it,' she went on huskily. 'I've learned things since living in their country. They scarcely ever marry for love. A man sees a girl he desires and promptly begins negotiations with her parents for a marriage. It's all purely sex, nothing else. Greek men are the most amorous in the world – and that should answer you if nothing else did.'

Tricia could not at first find anything to say to this and she merely stood there, a most troubled frown on her pretty face.

'If this is true, then I feel more blameworthy than ever,' she sighed at last, an appeal for pardon in her anxious eyes.

'It's not your fault,' Gale declared firmly, urged by the need for complete honesty. 'I wanted to marry him.'

Another silence fell, with Tricia staring at her friend as she tried to assess the real meaning of Gale's admission.

'You were in love with him, all the time?' she queried unbelievingly. 'But you always swore you'd never fall in love. When did you first know?'

Gale moistened her lips. She was aware that one or

two people were glancing their way, and because of what she had overheard she felt positive those glances held a thinly-veiled hint of amusement. She squirmed again and wished with all her heart she had not allowed impulse to bring her to England. Yet the next second she admitted she was glad she had learned about her husband's perfidy. She had no wish to be in the position of the trusting wife who was being betrayed without her knowledge. Far better to be in possession of the facts so that from now on she could arm herself against his charms. Dejection and sheer misery lay as a dead weight upon her as the future spread itself before her vision. No more lovemaking because she would refuse, and this of course meant the beginning of the end. Julius would undoubtedly find pleasure elsewhere.

'I didn't fall in love,' Gale admitted, jerked from her reverie by a small movement made by Tricia as a sign that she awaited an answer to her question. 'We both – both married for the same reason.'

Tricia blinked.

'I don't believe it!' she exclaimed. 'Men marry for that reason, I'll grant you – and perhaps as you say this is the case with most Greek men – but women never do!'

Gale had to smile in spite of her misery.

'You're not very realistic, Tricia. Women do. But they rarely admit it.'

'I think you fell in love with him,' stated Tricia, ignoring this. 'I know I should have, had the handsome, magnificent Julius Spiridon given me any attention. Why, you know very well that all the girls used to be crazy about him!'

'I didn't fall in love with him,' Gale denied. 'It was a

physical attraction on both sides, and we knew from the first that it wouldn't last.' She was speaking for Julius as well as herself, because she was firmly of the belief that she spoke the truth. 'It's ended sooner than I expected, and that's why I'm feeling so shattered. Never mind, though,' she added, managing to insert a lightness into her voice, 'the sooner the break the quicker the mend. Come on, I'm dying for a drink!'

CHAPTER NINE

GALE often wondered afterwards how she managed to remain at the Sims' for that week-end, adopting a lightness which none other than Tricia knew was on the surface only. And when it was time to leave Gale felt no better; she was going home to a father who did not care whether she was there or not, who would go out each evening and leave her alone. Still, there were only two such evenings to get over. After that her mother would be back home.

'Thought you were staying away until tomorrow,' snapped her father on coming home to a prepared meal and a glowing fire, which Gale had lighted because she herself had been icy cold all day.

'I said it depended on how I felt.'

'So it didn't come up to expectations—' He stopped suddenly and again she noticed that sharp intake of his breath, and its heaviness afterwards. Her eyes flickered over his face, but he looked to be in perfect health and she made no remark on what she had observed.

'I felt like coming home,' she told him.

'Well, I suppose you know what you want. By the time your mother returns it'll be time for you to be leaving again.'

She nodded, but reminded him that she did have three days. She had initially had the urge to go home earlier than planned, just to satisfy herself that Daphne was not on the island. Should she be away, then it would be clear who was the blonde Julius was with; should she be at home, then it would mean that Julius had yet another woman in tow – a woman who was also a blonde. But Gale checked the impulse to return to Patmos. She had come all this way specifically to see her mother and it was not very sensible to leave England without having at least a couple of days with her. Besides, she hoped to find her mother in a more communicative mood than previously. She hoped to learn more about this Jack, and whether he had been her mother's companion on the holiday.

Gale's hopes were to materialize, for after recovering from her surprise at finding her daughter at home waiting for her, Mrs. Davis opened up and talked. Gale learned that Jack had in fact been with her mother in Cornwall, but they had stayed in adjoining hotels.

'He paid for your holiday?'

'Yes, everything.' A pause and then, anxiously, and in the old rather deprecating manner, 'You're condemning me?'

'I'm not your judge,' replied Gale promptly. 'I think you've been a saint up till now. In any case, you've just said you stayed in separate hotels.'

'Yes, we did, and that's the truth. Jack's an honourable man. He knows how I feel about these modern ways and he understands.'

Gale smiled inwardly. How long would he understand, as her mother put it? He was a *man* – and that was sufficient for Gale to fasten the tag of insincerity upon him. She looked into her mother's glowing face and sighed. So innocent still, and so trusting. Heartache must come, and Gale could have wept for her.

'Tell me some more about him, darling,' she pressed. 'What does he look like? Is he a bachelor or a widower?' Probably married, her hardened heart added as a bitter light entered Gale's lovely eyes.

'He's been a widower for eight years, and never bothered with another woman until he met me three years ago.'

What a story! Gale said, successfully hiding her cynicism,

'How old is he?'

'Forty-eight. And he's as handsome as your Julius – almost. He's tall and stately . . . and he doesn't drink,' Mrs. Davis added significantly.

'His wife? Does he ever mention her?'

'He did once, and what I thought was so very nice,' went on Mrs. Davis with a smile reminiscent of a naïve teenager, 'was that he spoke affectionately of her. They were in love right to the end. He says that she knew for about a year that she was going to die and made him promise that he would marry again some day. He promised, just to please her, but he had no intention of doing so . . . not until he met me. But of course we can never marry. . . .' The low sweet voice trailed away to a sad silence and Gale found her throat blocked by a hurtful little lump which she could not dislodge. Presently, however, she did manage to ask what her mother's plans were.

'We haven't any.'

Gale nodded briefly, then wanted to know how they had met.

'It was the most unromantic thing!' Mrs. Davis's voice was light again, and she laughed to herself, musing privately for a fleeting moment. 'I came out of the supermarket loaded – had two of their carriers because I'd left my big basket on the bus, in an absent-minded moment. Well, you know how unreliable those bags are, and not *one* gave way, but both. All my shopping spread over the pavement! Everyone looking, so you can imagine how I felt?' Gale nodded and had to smile. So shy, her mother! This must have been the most embarrassing moment in her life. 'Some of the things rolled away into the gutter – like the scouring powder, which was in a drum. Then I'd bought vegetables and there were onions and tomatoes all rolling about.' She stopped and they both laughed together as they had not laughed for a long while.

'Go on,' urged Gale when she had recovered. 'This Jack came along, of course.'

'He stopped his car, but by that time all sorts of people were running about, picking things up. But I'd nowhere to put them. Jack promptly took over the situation, bringing out a large cardboard box from the car and telling the people to put the things into it. He then said he'd better take me home, which he did, and stayed for a cup of tea. The next day he called to see how I was—'

'To see how you were?' echoed Gale, puzzled. 'Were you hurt at all?' She could not recall her mother ever having anything wrong with her – not physically, that was.

'It was just an excuse! Surely you can see that. It became a regular thing for him to call, but after a few weeks I began to get worried about the neighbours. You know how women can put the wrong construction on things. Also, I felt guilty about the whole thing, and in addition I was getting far too fond of him – it's easy, Gale, when you've been starved of your husband's love for so long.' She stopped and glanced appealingly at her daughter.

'I understand, Mother,' Gale said softly, and her mother continued, telling her of the struggle and the decision to tell Jack he must not come again.

'I meant it to be a final break, but we could not, Gale, we just could not. Jack agreed that he mustn't keep coming to the house, but suggested we meet outside. This I flatly refused to do – but you already know that.'

'You obviously kept in touch, though.' Gale was beginning to revise her opinion of the man, who sounded sincere after all.

'Yes. We used to phone each other.'

'Each other? How could he phone you?'

'I used to be in the kiosk at a given time and he'd ring me there. He had an idea I hadn't much money and as he wanted to talk for a long time he said he'd rather phone me. However, I did phone him on occasions – in between his calls, just if I happened to get depressed.' She stopped and a small silence fell between them as each became absorbed in thought.

'This state of affairs must have gone on a long time,' commented Gale at last, and her mother nodded.

'Until you – I mean. . . .' She allowed her voice to trail away and a blush rose to her cheeks. How pretty she was, thought Gale. Love had done this . . . real love, not the shallow thing called desire on which her own marriage was based. These two had existed on spiritual love alone for three whole years. . . .

'Until I stayed at the lodge with Julius,' Gale finished for her, and the blush deepened and her mother looked away, as if unable to meet her daughter's eyes. These eyes narrowed. Gale was thinking about her conviction that her mother had been playing a part – that there was something dominating the whole business of her marriage, something mysterious and inexplicable.

'Yes, until you did that.' The words seemed forced

from her as Mrs. Davis continued to avoid her daughter's gaze. 'I felt justified in living my own life after that.'

'And so you met regularly?'

'That's right.'

'Tell me,' said Gale in a thoughtful sort of way, 'do you still believe I slept with Julius—?'

'Gale dear, please don't use these modern expressions!' her mother cut in, and Gale just had to laugh.

'What's so modern about that? You're fifty years behind the times, my pet. You haven't answered my question?' she added in an altered tone.

'I – I don't – don't know – exactly.'

'You don't?' Gale willed her mother to face her, but failed. 'Surely you know your own daughter?'

Her mother seemed lost for words; Gale was suddenly convinced that whatever she said her mother would not say the words Gale wanted her to. And this only added to the mystery. As the silence continued Gale changed the subject, reverting to Jack and asking if she could meet him.

'I was going to suggest that,' came the ready agreement. 'He's been wanting to meet you and Edward, but of course I'd *never* let him see Edward, who is so like me in that he dislikes these modern ways.' She stopped and gave a deprecating shrug in response to the amusement which had come swiftly to her daughter's eyes. 'You know what I mean?' she added at least.

'Of course, darling, but do go on.'

'I'll phone him this evening and we'll arrange to have dinner somewhere. He'll be so delighted at the idea of meeting you. He's even suggested he and I come out to Patmos for a holiday, just so he could meet you – and Julius, of course,' Mrs. Davis added as an afterthought.

'You go out to dinner with him regularly?' Gale asked, reflecting on this change in her mother's life and deciding she fully agreed with it.

'Yes, ever since we – I— Oh, dear, I'm not at all tactful.'

'Ever since the *episode* – shall we call it whenever reference to it is necessary?'

'You're laughing at me, dear, and that isn't at all like you, or kind!'

'It isn't at all like you – or kind – to brand me a no-good,' Gale couldn't help flashing back, but once again was denied the satisfaction of reading her mother's expression. 'I've only three days at most,' Gale reminded her, deciding there was no point in pursuing a subject which was unlikely to show profit. 'I want to be back before Julius.'

'Yes, of course, dear. We'll go out tomorrow evening.'

'Jack won't have anything else to do?'

A smile of confidence resulted from that question.

'If he had he'd cancel it,' came the answer, in tones possessing not the faintest thread of doubt.

'You certainly sound very confident of him, and happy.'

'I am happy – but of course not completely by any means. I'm grateful, though, to fate for sending Jack to me. He's making life bearable.' Gale listened and her eyes shadowed, but not for her mother this time. It was for herself she felt sympathy; she had lost so much in marrying for the reason she had married. She saw this now; she saw and admitted that spiritual love coupled with a deep mental attraction was the real foundation of marriage. Physical love was important – very important – but it must be cemented by the other two emotions, otherwise all must inevitably collapse.

Noticing this rather melancholy mood of preoccupation, Mrs. Davis suddenly asked, deep anxiety portrayed in her low attractive voice, 'Gale dearest – you are happy with Julius? You *must* be!' The exclamation came impulsively, as if actually torn from her, and Gale's head shot up and her expression was baffled while yet inquiring too.

'I'm happy – yes,' but without any marked enthusiasm, and to her amazement she actually saw her mother's eyes film over. She spoke, seeming to forget Gale's presence as she said,

'He loves you— You must be happy! Oh, if you're not, after what I did! It would be too awful – I'd never forgive myself for – for—' She broke off. Gale's eyes and ears were alert. She had the unshakeable conviction that she had been as close as she would ever be to solving the mystery of the events preceding her marriage.

'Go on, Mother,' she encouraged softly, but it was too late. Mrs. Davis with a swift recovery shook her head and fell silent for a space. But presently she became deeply troubled again and asked, this time looking deeply into Gale's eyes,

'You love him now? I know you didn't at first, but you've learned to since? Say you have, my dearest Gale, for otherwise I can never be happy again as long as I live.'

'I've learned to love him since our marriage,' returned Gale, intent only on assuaging his mother's conscience ... but it was with a sort of stunned disbelief that the truth hit her.

She had meant what she said.

The cosy little inn, set among a small grove of trees, and yet unblemished by the modernizing stampede of the brewers, was as homely as any cottage kitchen. A fire burned in the big black grate; crazy beams ran along an even crazier ceiling and disappeared into higgledy-piggledy walls. There was even a 'salt oven' which delighted everyone who saw it. Wall lights provided the only illumination – soft amber and intimate. Flowers grew in pots everywhere and soft strains of a waltz pervaded the small dining-room from some concealed instrument or box.

'Your usual table is reserved, madam.' The smiling waiter gestured towards the bar. 'You'll be having a drink first?'

'Of course.' Not a great deal of confidence in the tones, but enough to make Gale gasp. What a change had come over her mother! Love did more than put a glow in one's eyes, it seemed.

They were seated by the fire when suddenly Mrs. Davis's eyes lit up.

'That's his car outside. I know the sound of the engine.'

Gale's eyes went automatically to the window; dusk was falling and all she saw was the tall figure alight from the massive car and, closing the door, Jack locked it and strode away, out of sight round the side of the building, making for the entrance through which Gale and her mother had entered shortly before. Fleetingly Gale's thoughts went to her father; she could not help visualizing his expression were he to walk in and see his wife sitting there, flushed and lovely, waiting for her man friend to come into view.

A few seconds later Gale was looking up into the young, handsome face – a face so different from that of her father, whose dissolute pleasures over a long period had inevitably left their mark. This man was clean-living. There were no lines upon the firm bronzed skin, no nauseating odours of stale alcohol and nicotine emanating from his clothes. On the contrary there was the healthy smell of newly-laundered linen and the less commonplace one of after-shave lotion. His hair shone and so did his even white teeth; his grey worsted suit was immaculate and so were his suede shoes. He was an estate agent, her mother had told her, having his own business with branches in more than a dozen large towns.

'I'm very happy indeed to meet you, Gale.' He smiled as he spoke, and it was not difficult to see how he had come to win her mother's heart. His tones were low and cultured, his grip on her hand firm and friendly.

'That certainly goes for Gale, too,' Mrs. Davis could not help inserting on noting her daughter's expression.

'I don't know?' He looked down at Gale and waited a moment before adding, 'Gale should be allowed to speak for herself, my dear.'

'This is a pleasure,' she murmured with a smile. He saw that she was exceedingly relieved and laughed as he sat down beside her mother, beckoning for the waiter.

'I'm approved, I take it?' There was in his eyes the sort of satirical challenge Gale might have seen in those of her husband, had he been asking a similar question. Gale instantly gathered that although he hoped for her approval he certainly had no intention of begging for it. No wonder her mother had fallen for him! He had just about everything, even to that certain degree of arrogance that is an essential facet of supreme masculinity.

Gale just had to say,

'Is my approval really important?' She found she was experiencing a certain awkwardness as she did not know what to call him.

'Your mother would be troubled if you decided you didn't like me.'

She shook her head, voicing the spontaneous thought that came directly upon this statement.

'I couldn't possibly dislike you.'

Faintly he inclined his head; the dark brown hair caught the light from the back of the bar, and it shone with bronze glints and the merest suggestion of a grey strand here and there.

'Thank you, Gale. I can most sincerely say the same about you. I'd heard all about you, of course—' He broke off and smiled affectionately at her mother. 'Yes, I've heard all about both you and your brother. Two of the best children in the world—'

'Jack, dear!'

'All right, I shan't embarrass either of you further.' His drink had come; he pressed them to have another, but they refused and both picked up their glasses as Jack said, very serious all at once, 'Let us drink to the future . . . and to our happiness.' Gale put the glass to her lips, but she was suddenly too full to drink. Where was this elusive thing called happiness? It could be snatched and caught – but it so often slipped away before it was safely ensnared . . . and it mocked as it escaped. What happiness was there for the three sitting here, in this intimate room in an old-world inn hidden away, the trysting-place where lovers could at least hope to meet with some degree of safety. In dreamy musings Gale saw these two, meeting here in their secret place which somehow they had found – and perhaps others like them had also found it. Dimly-lit, discreetly-screened tables – just five in all. It might have been designed exclusively for clandestine meetings.

'You're a long way off, Gale.' Jack's voice brought her back and she smiled at him across the table. The firelight caught her lovely features in its mellow saffron glow and she saw the gleam of appreciation enter his eyes. 'Where were you? Back in Greece with your husband?'

She swallowed, wondering just how much her mother had told him. Nothing, she decided on reflection. He would have wanted to know why she was here all alone, though, and her mother would have told him over the phone that Julius was in Munich on business and so Gale had seized the opportunity of coming home.

'In a way, yes.' It was a white lie and she felt her colour rise faintly. 'I was thinking about – happiness.'

A small silence fell and Gale sought her mother's eyes. They were shadowed, but not too much so. She was grateful for what she had – grateful and even satisfied. Gale shifted her gaze to the man who was so attractive that it seemed impossible he hadn't been ensnared before now. Many women must have been attracted to him, as they were to Julius. But he had not philandered. . . . The thought that her husband had philandered hurt abominably and she tried to thrust away that admission of yesterday, tried to tell herself it was not true. She had not fallen in love with her husband – she wouldn't be so utterly foolish. Hadn't she vowed never to put herself in so vulnerable a position a second time? And hadn't she remained immune for over five years?

Bitterness flooded over her as the truth prevailed, crushing these feeble protests and forcing her to face up to reality. She had fallen in love with Julius ... and had been let down for a second time. She deserved all she got!

Two days after the cosy little dinner Gale was back in Patmos, waiting for Julius's return. He had informed Apollo earlier that he would be arriving about six in the evening and this information was conveyed to Gale the moment she stepped into the villa. She had thanked Apollo, and then by subtle questioning had managed to elicit from him the further information that Daphne was also away from home. And now Gale was waiting, pale but resolved, to impart her own information – to her husband. She would tell him at once that the marriage was at an end. He could have Daphne, could spend all his time in Paris with her if he wished. Gale would convince him she didn't care.

He came by taxi from the harbour; she watched its slow approach as it covered the last length of drive and came to a standstill close to where she stood, on the patio, in the swiftly-fading twilight. With his customary elegant grace Julius alighted, paid the driver, left him to deal with the luggage, with the help of Apollo who had come from the side of the villa, and, taking the steps three at a time, he stood close to his wife, looking down into her pale face with an expression of sardonic amusement.

'Miss me, my dear?'

Her eyes blazed, seeming to light up her whole countenance.

'Why should I?' she countered, keeping a hold on that fury that threatened to burst into an all-consuming conflagration. 'Did you have an enjoyable time in Munich?'

'I didn't go for enjoyment, you know that.' He was puzzled and frowning. His voice took on an edge of crispness as he said, 'What's wrong with you? I expected an eager welcome and what do I get? A wife with a face like a thundercloud. You did miss me – now just you own to it.'

Her fists clenched. Temper raged, but it was bitter pain and disillusionment that caused the tears to form behind her eyes. How attractive he was, even now, with that distinctive hair and the lines of perfection forming dark and arrogant features. Hollows beneath the high cheekbones gave an added leanness to his face; his eyes seemed darker than ever – almost black. With a sudden flood of shame she admitted she wanted nothing more than to feel his arms about her . . . his hand on her heart. . . .

Thoughts like this gave colour to her face and his frown deepened at this swift and incomprehensible change.

'I'm sorry to disappoint you, Julius,' she managed with well-feigned lightness. 'I too have been away. I went home.'

'You did?' He shrugged. 'So you didn't miss me, after all?'

'Quite right,' with a sort of acid sweetness, 'I didn't.'

'I see.' He appeared to be set back somewhat by this news and she thought, 'It would almost seem he went away specifically to test me, to discover whether or not I would miss him.'

But of course that was not the reason for his going away. He had a very different reason altogether.

'Mother sends her regards,' she said, watching him

closely. His face was an unreadable mask and all he said was,

'That's nice of her. Thank her when you write.' His voice retained its crisp edge, but he seemed strangely tired, she thought. Tired . . . well, that was to be expected!

She said, on an impulse that could not be checked,

'Daphne's been away too.'

His eyes widened and his regard became baffled.

'Well?'

She stared at him in disbelief. Not the glimmer of guilt in his eyes, no swift start of shame followed by the adoption of a guarded manner. How well he did it!

'I believe she's been in Paris.'

Silence. At last Gale felt she had shaken him. And yet, deep within her, the longing for him was wildly clamouring to be heard and a warning voice telling her that, should she bring matters to a head now, she would never know his nearness again . . . never feel the command of that lean body against hers, the complete mastery of those lips, persuading, demanding, conquering. . . . With all her heart she wanted him and as the battle raged within her she heard him say, the most odd inflection in his voice,

'Is there any special reason why you've mentioned where Daphne's been?' A tentative question and a sort of anxious wait for her reply. The obvious answer flashed to her lips, only to be suppressed. She tried again with the same result. Tears pricked the backs of of her eyes, fighting for release, and she brought down her lids, for comfort. She knew her husband watched her closely and she was overwhelmingly grateful for the diminishing twilight that pervaded the vine-draped patio, clothing it with shadows.

'No, Julius,' she managed at last, a tremor in her voice. 'There was no special reason.' She stopped, panic seizing her in case he himself should carry the subject further – carry it to the point where there could be no retreat for either of them. If he had tired of her already then he would not mind in the least if exposure were to be his. He was regarding her with such an odd expression. He knew he'd been in Paris with Daphne, and the very fact of Gale's mentioning that Daphne had been in Paris must strike him as pointed, which it was intended to be, with regret following swiftly. 'I just mentioned it for – for interest – because I've always wanted to – to go there.'

His eyes narrowed and for one frightened moment she felt he would come right out and make her explain the reason in a more credible way. But all at once he seemed to relax and she breathed freely again. Yet her relief was not the pure uncomplicated sensation she would have wished for. Julius had been as anxious as she not to lead the way to the point where *finis* must inevitably be written. This meant that he had not yet tired of her, that desire lingered still with him as it did with her. And so the reprieve, though welcome, afforded her scant satisfaction. She looked up at Julius, and wondered if the dampness on her lashes was visible. She thought not, because surely he could have commented. Instead he asked, softly and with interest,

'How do you know that Daphne's been in Paris?'

She had known the question would come, and was prepared for it. But she averted her head as the lie left her lips.

'Apollo mentioned it. It was he who told me Daphne was away on holiday.'

'I see. . . .' The faint dropping of the voice left her a

trifle worried in case he should question Apollo, who had never even mentioned Paris. But her anxiety soon faded; Julius was above talking in this way to his servants.

CHAPTER TEN

THEY had followed the path of the pilgrims, climbing up to the grotto where John the Apostle wrote the Apocalypse, and now they were standing in the courtyard of the Byzantine monastery, watching a black-bearded Greek Orthodox priest talking to a group of people who had come from the white cruise ship anchored just off Skala, the port of Patmos, so tiny that passengers from the liners had to be brought ashore by launch.

'He's happy – quite in his element.' Julius spoke to his wife, his tones cool and impersonal, just as they had been for the past three days, ever since he returned from his business trip. 'The tourists bring money to the monastic coffers.'

Gale glanced at him. He wore a small but exquisite gold cross, she knew. Many Greek men wore such religious emblems, but with Julius it seemed oddly at variance with his character. He was so hard, so concerned with practicalities.

'Is the monastery very rich?' Her own tones were cool, matched to his. But it hurt now to speak like this. She yearned for tenderness to creep into their relationship. It never would, of course; even desire seemed to have died – at least on Julius's part, as he had not come to her since his return. Strangely, her great longing for him troubled her far less than her unrequited love, the strength of which was causing her to question her self-professed conviction that she had married him for desire alone. At the time, love had not even occurred to her, but now she was beginning to wonder if his deep and potent attraction had awakened in her something far more powerful than desire. Often she would think of Daphne, and jealousy would surge with such force that she felt she must come out with her knowledge – just to discover her husband's reaction, and to endeavour to find out just how much Daphne meant to him.

'Very rich indeed,' Julius was saying in answer to her question. 'It owns land in several Greek islands and also in Cyprus.' He suggested they go on to the terrace and admire the magnificent view – the island of Leros and the tiny islands of Arki and Lipsi could be seen from there, he told her. He sounded bored, she thought, and bit her lip till it hurt. It seemed impossible that her attraction for him had waned so swiftly. Was he lost in the memory of Paris, and Daphne? It was very plain to Gale that the other girl could give him much more than his wife could . . . and yet, if this were so, Gale was thinking a moment later, then why hadn't he married her? It could of course be the old reason – that a Greek never married a woman he had already made love to. Yes, that appeared to be the feasible explanation. Sighing, Gale shook her head, for a dart of memory had brought back her conviction that some mystery attached to the events leading up to the marriage.

'What was the sigh for?' Her husband's deep and pleasing voice intruded and she glanced up. She might have known he would not miss that little outward sign of her frustration. 'You appear to be troubled about something?'

'No, I'm not,' she began, then stopped, aware of the curious expression on Julius's face. He was more than ordinarily interested in her reply; he also appeared rather satisfied with himself, she suddenly noticed.

'Why are you looking so pleased?' The question was out before she could check it and he frowned as if annoyed by it. But his tone was affable enough when he spoke.

'I wasn't aware I did look pleased. You haven't answered my question.'

'Your question?'

Again he frowned. It was clear that all that interested him at the moment was the nature of her response to his inquiry.

'I asked if you were troubled about something?'

They had reached the terrace and Gale stared out, away to the north where the Fourni Islands shone in the bright sunlight and the larger outline of Ikaria appeared like some tranquil vessel riding at anchor.

Gale moved restlessly, conscious of her husband's sustained interest and his slight impatience at the delay in her reply. He would insist on hearing it, she knew, and evasion seemed imperative, for her present mood was such that she was very close to confessing that she knew he had been with Daphne in Paris – or, more correctly, reminding him that she knew. And this would occasion the sort of scene that could very well lead to the end of the marriage, since Julius would be forced to admit that Daphne still held a profound attraction for him. In these circumstances Gale would – if she had any pride at all – have no alternative than to make as dignified an exit as possible. She would have to return to England, to her home. Her father would jeer, while her mother would be heartbroken, for there was no doubt at all in Gale's mind that her mother desired above all things that her daughter should be happy. No, Gale could not force such a situation and she said, with haste now, as if she must make up for the time lost, and in so doing allay any suspicions Julius might have that she was searching for a plausible lie with which to answer his question and so satisfy him.

'I am troubled, yes – about Mother.'

'Your mother?' Was it imagination, Gale wondered, or had her reply really disappointed him? Most certainly it had erased that satisfied look from his face. Was it possible that he had assumed she had been troubled about them – her husband and herself? If so, he had been right, of course, and as Gale dwelt for a time on this new idea, she found her heartbeats increasing rapidly, as it would seem that he wanted to bring their marriage into discussion. Did he want to talk about a separation . . . or about trying to make something of the marriage? Of the two possibilities Gale could think only of the former, because of what she had learned about his being in Paris with Daphne. Her heartbeats raced as fear mounted. To lose him. . . .

'I told you all about her – and the holiday – and that we all met.' Gale spoke huskily, fighting tears which were striving for release. 'I'm – I'm worried because she isn't happy.'

He made no comment for a while, but stared down into her eyes, probing as if he would discover whether or not she was lying about the reason for her troubled sigh of a few moments ago. At length he shrugged as if accepting her words as the truth.

'She never appeared particularly unhappy to me,' he said at last. 'She seemed resigned that they could never marry, and grateful that she had Jack at all.'

This was true; Gale had reached the same conclusion herself, but of course she could not now inform her husband of this.

'It's all very sad,' she murmured, absorbed in her own thoughts now, and for the moment forgetting about personal problems as she saw her mother going on and on, living apart from the man she loved. Would Jack remain faithful, and satisfied with such an arrangement? With a little catch of fear Gale wondered if he would ever let her mother down

'In a way it's sad,' agreed Julius, but added, 'At least they have love to help them along.' He sounded bitter, she thought, glancing, swiftly at him. Could it be possible that he wanted love in his life? – he who had always given her the impression that his needs could be satisfied by physical attraction alone?

He turned from her and gazed out at the view. Moments later he was pointing towards Leros, and the two tiny islands of Arki and Lipsi. The conversation became impersonal and even cool. A great rift had come between them by the time they returned to the villa.

'For you, Mrs. Julius.' Kate looked a trifle worried as she handed Gale the cable. 'It come one minute after you go out, but I can't find you when I run along the road.'

Gale and Julius were in the hall; he stood watching as with trembling hands Gale opened out the paper and read the brief message.

'What's wrong?' he asked on noting the colour leave her face. 'Your mother . . .?'

'Father. He's had a stroke.' Automatically she held out the cable to him. 'I must go home.' She felt lost and alone, just as on the occasion when she was in the house on her own, after having looked forward so eagerly to seeing her mother again. If only Julius would offer to go to England with her . . . but he would not. He would most probably welcome her absence. It gave him the opportunity to be with Daphne. . . . Dejection had been engulfing Gale all the way home and now, despite her efforts at control, she put her face in her hands and wept.

'You may go, Kate.' Gale heard her husband's voice, low and strangely tight. 'Come,' he said gently, 'crying won't help.' Unexpectedly he put an arm around her shoulders and guided her into the living-room. 'Sit down. I'll get you a drink.'

She shook her head, looking urgently at him.

'I must make inquiries about a flight. You read – read the message. Father's dangerously ill—'

'Do as you're told, Gale,' he interrupted quietly but firmly. 'I shall make all the necessary arrangements for our flight.'

Unbelievingly she stared at him, blinking away the tears.

'You're coming with me?'

He raised his brows, in censure.

'Surely you expected me to come with you?'

Gale moved her head, in a bewildered gesture. But words would not come. She was too full to speak just now, not only because of the news she had received from home, but also because of the flood of relief that swept through her.

Contrary to her conclusions, Julius had not grasped this opportunity of being with Daphne.

After bringing her a drink and making her sit down on the couch with it, he went off to telephone. There was a flight from Piraeus the following day, he told her on his return. They would have to catch the ferry which was leaving in a couple of hours' time.

'We'll be on board through part of the night, but I've managed to get a cabin.'

'Thank you, Julius.' She had not touched the brandy he had brought her and now he sternly ordered her to drink it.

'You'll feel better,' he assured her, and in fact she did realize she needed a drink. Would her father live to be a burden on her mother for the rest of her life? Or would he . . .? Gale shivered violently.

'I don't want him to die,' she whispered almost to herself. 'He's been wicked, but—' She glanced up to Julius's face, tears springing to her eyes again. 'He's my father, and – and – when Edward and I were young he did sometimes play games with us.'

Julius said nothing, but as she watched his changing expression she knew he was considering that her father had never really done what a father should do for his children. And for a fleeting moment Gale forgot everything as she saw, in imagination, her husband with children. He would be a good father, and kind – but then Greek men had a reputation for being inordinately fond of children.

'Don't think about his dying,' Julius said gently. 'We don't know just how serious his condition is—'

'Mother would never exaggerate,' she cut in.

'I agree, but nevertheless, we mustn't look on the black side.' Although he spoke gravely his voice had a firm edge as he added, 'You're not to let your imagination run away with you, Gale. I shall be angry if you make yourself ill. Do you understand?'

She nodded, wondering at the meek way in which she received this stern injunction. Yet it was pleasant to be managed, she was secretly admitting as, taking her empty glass, Julius gave her a gentle push so that she rested against the soft cushions at her back. So strange it was, this gentleness in one so superior and arrogant. And deep concern was there, on that stern set countenance. Gale did not get round to asking herself the reason for that concern, for her thoughts switched back to her father, and she was wishing with all her heart that she had not been so unfriendly with him on her recent visit. She told herself she should have been more conscious of that gasping for breath which she had noticed – not once, but twice. Filled with remorse she told Julius of this, tears springing to her eyes as she spoke. His mouth set for a moment before he said,

'You have nothing to blame yourself for, Gale, so stop doing so! There was nothing you could have done—'

'I could have advised him to see a doctor.'

'Would he have taken that advice?'

Reluctantly she admitted that in all probability he would not have done so.

'I could have warned Mother, though,' she added, and heard an impatient sigh issue from her husband's lips. His tone was rather dangerously quiet as he said,

'That's enough, Gale. Invariably there is self-blame when tragedies like this occur – and more often than not there isn't the least need for that self-blame. I've just told you, I shall be angry with you if you make yourself ill.'

Gale kept her thoughts to herself after that; and she was forced to eat some lunch because Julius's stern eye was on her the whole time. When lunch was over they had only a few minutes to spare before being driven by Apollo to Skala, where they boarded the ferry. It was only when they were being taken to their cabin that she remembered he had ordered only one – not two, as she would have expected. At the time of his mentioning it she had not been in a fit state of mind for it to register properly. She looked up at him as they entered and he closed the door.

'Do you mind?' He slanted her a look, but it was one she could not read.

'I'd rather be with you,' she admitted after a slight pause during which she formed the hope that he would not misunderstand her meaning. 'For comfort,' she decided to add, just to make sure.

He smiled faintly then but made no comment. And much later, when she was in her bunk, he tucked the rug around her and after dropping a light kiss on her forehead slipped into his own bunk and snapped off the light.

Mr. Davis was lying in the bed, his eyes glazed, his mouth unmoving. Gale stood looking down at him and wondered at the change in his appearance. One side of his face was drawn up in an ugly, grotesque way that made her shudder inwardly.

'The doctor should be here directly,' Mrs. Davis's voice was scarcely audible; her face was white, her eyes shaded with guilt. Earlier she had claimed that this was all her fault, that it was brought on by her going out, and not telling her husband where she went. 'He's been fretting,' she said, but Gale could not agree.

'Had he been fretting he just couldn't have continued to go out himself,' she had to say, for it was wrong that her mother should shoulder the blame.

'I'll never forgive myself.' Mrs. Davis spoke as if her daughter's words had not been uttered. 'I should have given Jack up.'

Julius, who was also in the room, became almost as stern with Mrs. Davis as he had with Gale the previous afternoon when she too had fallen to blaming herself.

'No guilt attaches to either of you,' he said, his glance moving to Gale and then back to her mother. 'If I might speak frankly, it's my firm opinion that this present condition of your husband has been brought about entirely through the life he has led. Our bodies must inevitably succumb if we strain their resources past the limit to which they are meant to go.'

Logical words and, Mrs. Davis later admitted, ones which had been spoken by the doctor on the day the stroke occurred.

'Not that every stroke is the result of over-indulgence,' the doctor had said, 'but in this case I'm bound to say that your husband has driven himself to destruction.'

Gale dwelt on these words now as she stood with her mother beside the bed, looking down at the man lying there. Every night for as long as Gale could remember he had been out drinking, and it was not at all unusual for him to return home as late as four o'clock in the morning. This, as often as not, when he had to be at the university at nine.

'Shall I go, Mother?' Gale put the question as the doctor walked into the room, having let himself in at the front door.

'No, dear, please stay.'

Ten minutes later the doctor had gone, leaving Gale and her mother with the news that Mr. Davis had only a few hours to live.

'You've been so very kind, Julius,' Mrs. Davis was saying a week after the funeral. 'It's so comforting to have someone to lean on, someone who sees to things with such unobtrusive efficiency. I think my daughter is a most fortunate young woman.' She glanced affectionately at Gale as she spoke. But Gale avoided her eyes, for she was not at all sure that she was fortunate, not with things being as they were between Julius and herself. True, he had not seized the opportunity to be with Daphne, but Gale had reached the conclusion that despite his gentleness and concern, his decision to accompany her to England had stemmed from a sense of duty alone. It was in keeping with his character for him to consider it his duty to come with his wife, and the more Gale reflected on this the more dejected she became. This dejection gave rise to the nagging conviction that Julius would, if the truth were known, far rather have stayed behind with Daphne. She lifted her head to glance at him, saw him frown and could not decide whether it was owing to her mother's words or to some secret thought of his own.

'It was nothing,' he said. 'Obviously at such times as these one must make oneself useful.'

'You've done everything for us, Julius, and I do thank you—' Mrs. Davis broke off as her son-in-law lifted a hand. 'Very well, I shan't mention it again, but I shall remember.'

They were dining out, at the small cosy inn where they were to meet Jack. Mrs. Davis would have refused Jack's suggestion, when he called four days after the funeral, but again it was Julius who took over, saying at once that it would be pleasant for them all to get together before he and his wife returned to Greece. They had stayed on for two reasons: firstly, Gale had no desire to leave her mother too soon, and in this Julius was in full agreement, and secondly, Julius had decided to conduct some business while in England, and the day after the funeral he had gone to London for a couple of days. Tomorrow Julius was visiting a few friends and then they were catching the early morning plane the following day.

Jack was already there when they arrived. It was the first social meeting between the two men and on seeing them together Gale was struck by the likeness in physique and bearing, both looking a hundred per cent fit and both possessing a similar air of confidence and authority. It was soon evident that they were to get along, and before the evening was over Julius had extended an invitation for Jack and Mrs. Davis to stay with him and Gale at the villa.

'It's an open invitation,' he added. 'I don't expect you'll wish to come just now.' He glanced at Gale, for she had given a slight start, and as their eyes met briefly she knew he read deep and profound relief in hers. In his she read faint surprise. It was clear that if she herself had doubts about the future, her husband had none – at least, it was plain that he wasn't contemplating a separation just yet.

For a short moment Gale despised herself; had she any pride at all she would not be wanting to remain with a husband who had already been unfaithful to her ... and yet she knew for sure that she would never leave him by her own design.

The following day he went off, leaving Gale and her mother to spend a few hours alone. He would return in time for the evening meal, Julius promised.

Mrs. Davis had been wearing an anxious expression for several days; Gale had put it down to the strain which could be expected at this time, but as she and Gale sat, during the afternoon, she asked Gale a question she had put to her on a previous occasion.

'Gale dear, you are happy with Julius?'

Gale looked at her, noting the same deeply-troubled expression she had seen before. The mystery seemed to be looming up again.

'Would it trouble you very much if I said I was not happy?' she inquired in a level tone, while keeping her eyes fixed upon her mother's face, a face that went a trifle pale as the words left Gale's lips.

'Yes – indeed it would! You must know that – you're happy,' she said urgently. 'You are! Say it!'

What would happen were she to tell the truth? – were she to say no, she was not happy? Nothing would have given Gale more satisfaction than to say this, just to see whether or not her mother would then decide to be more communicative. But Gale could not hurt her at this time, and to relieve her anxiety she said,

'I am happy, darling, so don't look so troubled. What makes you ask the question anyway?'

A small sigh, but relief instantly took the shadows from Mrs. Davis's eyes.

'You don't *look* happy – not like a bride should; I couldn't bear it if you were regretting the marriage, not after . . . after . . .'

'Yes, Mother?' prompted Gale softly.

'Well . . . after my insistence that you marry Julius. However, as long as you're not regretting the marriage, and you're perfectly happy, then let's not talk about it any more.' She was eager to change the subject and before Gale could speak she went on to say, 'Would it seem very wrong if Jack and I came over to spend Christmas with you and Julius?'

'Certainly not. Why shouldn't you spend Christmas with us?'

'It would be quite all right for me to do so, but – Jack?'

'You deserve to be happy,' Gale told her gently. 'You haven't a thing to reproach yourself for. You've been a good, faithful wife, and were even willing to remain with Father even though you loved someone else.' Gale shook her head. 'There's no reason at all why you should not come together.'

'Later – we'll be married.'

'Of course.'

'Edward wouldn't approve of my bringing Jack—'

'Darling, it isn't as if you're going to sleep together—'

'Gale! Oh, I do wish you were a little more delicate! Young people say the most embarrassing things!'

Gale had to laugh despite the solemnity which hung over the house.

'You're still old-fashioned, aren't you, darling? Perhaps Jack will eventually bring you out.'

'I don't want to be brought out, as you put it. I'm all right as I am.'

'Julius thinks you're old-fashioned, but admires you for having ideals.'

Her mother coloured prettily.

'I do like your Julius, Gale. You're so very lucky that he fell in love with you—' She broke off swiftly on noting her daughter's changing expression. Gale was about to speak, but at that moment the bell rang and Jack appeared. He had been looking at a property in a nearby road and so decided to drop in to see Mrs. Davis. As it was almost tea time he was invited to stay, and just as he was leaving Julius drove up in a taxi. Gale gave a sigh. Having decided once and for all to tackle her mother outright, she was to be thwarted, it seemed.

Very noticeable was her husband's expression, and the strange manner in which he regarded her throughout the meal. When it was over, and they were drinking coffee in the sitting-room, she was still acutely aware of his curious attitude, and the glances he gave her certainly conveyed the fact of his having something on his mind – something which affected her as well as himself.

He spoke immediately they were in their room, having said goodnight to Gale's mother, who had also gone to bed.

'Can it possibly be that you overheard Dave Ingham a second time?' he inquired without preamble, and his answer was received when Gale gave a visible start of surprise.

'You've been with him today?'

'I asked you a question, Gale.' Soft words and a little impatient sigh following. Gale nodded and averted her head, remembering that Julius had admonished her for eavesdropping on that previous occasion. 'What did you overhear?'

No answer, and Julius repeated his question, tilting her face up at the same time and keeping his finger under her chin until she spoke.

'I heard – heard his friend say – say. . . .' She twisted away, shaking her head. 'I'm not telling you! I don't want to talk about it—' She stopped as Julius took hold of her shoulders and swung her round to face him. His jaw was set and stern – but there was not the least sign of guilt portrayed on his dark and handsome features.

'Why don't you want to talk about it?' he demanded, yet afforded her no opportunity of answering as he continued, 'There can be only one reason – fear! You're afraid of the showdown which you have concluded will break up our marriage. Correct me if I'm wrong.'

She looked up, pale and trembling as she nodded, and huskily admitted that she had in fact avoided a showdown. 'Do you realize what that confession really means? Do you know what it has conveyed to me?'

Puzzled, she shook her head.

'You're talking in riddles, Julius.'

'You overheard Professor Ingham and his friend

talking about me – saying I'd been in Paris with a blonde—'

'The other man said that, but – but Dave was amused – I could tell by his tone.'

Julius's eyes glinted.

'I don't think it matters from whom you heard it!' A slight pause and then, 'So you believed that of me?' Something in his tone jerked her senses, and this in turn caused her pulse to quicken. She said breathlessly,

'It isn't true?'

His mouth went tight, and the grip on her arms began to hurt.

'It's true that I was in Paris, and also true that I was with a woman. But that woman was not Daphne – nor anyone else of importance,' he added on noting her face fall at his mention of a woman. 'She happened to be the wife of the business associate with whom I was staying, and as both she and I were going into town that particular morning we travelled together in her car. After she had parked it we walked no more than a couple of hundred yards together before she went off to the hairdressers and I to the office where I had a business appointment.' He paused a moment, almost glowering at her. 'Anything else you would like me to explain?' Despite his expression there was in his voice a certain something which Gale analysed as relief. He at least was glad that the air was being cleared.

'You said you were going to Munich,' she reminded him at last, moving away as his grip slackened.

'That's where I did go. The Paris trip resulted from talks I had there. I *am* in the travel business, Gale, and it's quite normal for me to move around.'

Deflated, Gale was silent for a time.

'Daphne was away at the same time as you,' she murmured presently. 'You must admit it was an odd coincidence?' Scanning his face, she saw the censure return to it.

'I had no idea of that,' he returned stiffly. And he added, his eyes glinting dangerously, 'You lied when you said Apollo had told you Daphne had been in Paris, but I didn't know this until today, when Dave began pulling my leg about a blonde I'd been with. I naturally realized that there was some connection between this and the fact of your mentioning Daphne had been in Paris. I soon learned from Dave that I'd been discussed at Tricia's party and it wasn't difficult to conclude that you had overheard this conversation. You must have done so, since no one was going to tell you outright that your husband was in Paris with another woman.'

Diverted for a moment, she said tartly,

'Indeed no! Men are nothing if not loyal!'

He laughed then, and received a glinting look for his trouble.

'So much is explained now,' he said, causing her to give an involuntary little gasp as tenderness she would never have expected entered his voice. 'I was astounded at the reception you gave me on my return.' He paused a moment, regarding her with an all-examining gaze. 'I went away primarily to discover whether or not you'd miss me,' he told her, and her eyes opened very wide.

'I gained that very impression!' she exclaimed.

'If you had missed me,' he continued, ignoring the interruption, 'I'd have known that you loved me, and,' he added in an even, measured tone, 'I'd have responded by telling you that your love was returned.'

She stared, unable to believe her ears. Her lips formed a little 'Oh,' of dismay which merely had the effect of bringing a flicker of amusement to her husband's eyes. She would have spoken again, would have inquired breathlessly if he really meant what he said but she was denied the opportunity as he went on to say, in a tone of affected heartlessness,

'See what you missed by your cleverness? You'd overheard someone say I'd been in Paris with a blonde; you'd learned from Apollo that Daphne had been away – *away*, mark you! No one had told you she was in Paris, but with typical feminine distrust you put two and two together and made the pattern which satisfied you – the pattern of an unfaithful husband who had told you he was going to Munich alone when in fact he was going to Paris with his ex-girl-friend. I expect you wallowed in self-pity; I can imagine your deciding to have a showdown – in fact, you started to do so and then changed your mind. Because, Gale, you were afraid of losing me— No, don't you dare deny it! I certainly won't deny that I myself was afraid of losing you, and that was why I did not pursue the matter. Had you received me differently on my return,' he continued, ignoring her several little gestures of imploration for him to cease this tormenting speech, 'I might then have told you why I married you.'

'Why ...?' Bewilderedly she stared at him. 'It wasn't – wasn't for – desire?'

Julius regarded her in silence for a long moment before, in the tenderest voice she had ever heard in the whole of her life, he told her he had fallen in love with her almost on sight. But he was honest enough to add that marriage had not immediately occurred to him; he was initially interested in having an affair with her. She blushed and he caught her to him, kissing her with the ardour she had so desired on the day of his return from Paris.

'Dearest,' he whispered when at last he took his lips from hers, 'there was only one answer to my question of a short while ago. Let me hear that answer.'

She was too full to speak; this was like some miracle and although there were still vital questions she herself must ask, she merely lifted her face again, inviting his kiss. Julius obliged, his dark eyes triumphant in a way that thrilled her through and through because it was the triumph of love returned.

'You mean,' she managed at last, 'the question about what my confession had conveyed to you?'

'Playing for time?' Julius slanted her a look which held a great deal of amusement. 'Or merely being coquettish? Is it necessary – when I know very well that you love me?'

Rosily she coloured, but because she was now so very sure of him she took the risk of saying,

'There could have been an altogether different reason for my avoiding the showdown. We married for desire, remember, and so it could have been desire that made me reluctant to do anything which might bring about an end to the marriage—' She was cut short as, roughly, he shook her.

'Desire! Don't you dare say that! It was love – just as it was with me. And what's this about marrying for desire? I've just told you I married you for love.'

'Of course. . . .' She became thoughtfully silent. 'I know now, Julius, that it was love with me too.'

He nodded, but said he wished he could have been sure of that before now.

'You see,' he went on to explain, 'the thought that you had no real love for me naturally resulted in my adopting an attitude of restraint. I could not bring myself to tell you the truth – not believing as I did that you had no love for me.' He bent his dark head and kissed her, tenderly. And for a while they were content to stand close together, in the silence of their room.

'Mother,' said Gale eventually, deciding to clear up the mystery she knew had existed at the time of her marriage. 'She acted in a way totally out of character by forcing the marriage on me.'

Julius answered without hesitation, telling Gale that, although her mother had sent for him, it was only to discover the truth, to find out whether or not he and Gale had really been together at the lodge.

'I told her the truth; she was filled with remorse, saying she had misjudged you and told you she could only forgive you if you had been contemplating marriage. Well, beloved, it was a chance too good to miss, for at that time I could not hope to meet with a favourable answer if I asked you to marry me. You were bent on remaining a spinster, remember?' Amusement edged his voice and a shaky laugh escaped her.

'I remember, Julius,' she said, and asked him to go on with his story.

'I had several talks with your mother, convincing her that I loved you to distraction—'

'No,' she interrupted firmly. 'Not to distraction! Not you!'

'To distraction, my dearest life – and don't interrupt! After a great deal of persuasion I finally managed to get her co-operation—'

'So *that* was it! A conspiracy? I understand everything now!'

'You do? Well, there's no need for me to say more.'

'Yes, please tell me the rest.'

'She agreed to my suggestion that she threaten to run off with Jack—'

'You suggested it? And she agreed! Julius, you must

have put on the charm to make my mother agree to a thing like that!'

'I had convinced her that we were meant for one another. I promised I'd make you love me. I told her your whole life's happiness was in her hands, and that if she refused to co-operate, and later you made an unhappy marriage – or perhaps kept to your intention of never marrying at all – it would be entirely her fault—'

'Oh, how could you! My poor mother!' She pulled away from him. 'How dreadfully unkind. I don't know how you do it!'

'You wish I hadn't?' he asked curiously.

'Yes – no – I mean. . . .'

He laughed and resolutely pulled her to him again.

'Let's have no more of that nonsense. You're inordinately grateful to me for bullying your poor mother, as you call her.'

She bristled.

'What a pompous man you are! I always knew it—' The rest, which she did not mean anyway, was smothered by his kiss.

'I knew Mother was too shy to ask you to marry me,' said Gale when at last she was given the opportunity to speak. 'I should have known at once that the idea had not been hers.' She told Julius that she had been conscious all the while of some mystery, mentioning the slips her mother had made, but which had not helped Gale to clear up that mystery. 'She seemed quite distraught, on one occasion, when she thought I might not be happy.'

'You didn't let her know you weren't happy?'

She shook her head.

'I couldn't – but oh, I was so frustrated all the while!'

'Woman's innate curiosity, eh?' he laughed. 'I expect you were angry with everyone concerned – when you were forced to marry me, I mean?'

'I was, yes; but, strangely,' she added on a reflective note, 'I was never as angry with Mother as with anyone else. It must have been because, subconsciously, I really was glad the marriage was forced upon me by her.'

Julius merely shrugged his shoulders and as Gale pondered on various incidents she asked him suddenly why he had not revealed his anger, that day on the beach, when she was rude to Daphne.

'You never said a word until we'd left her,' Gale added, looking curiously at him. He held her away, his eyes glinting, and Gale wondered vexedly why she had been so foolish as to bring this up.

'Rude to Daphne? It was the order you gave *me* that got you into trouble!' Gale nodded, and averted her head and for a long moment Julius left her to her own thoughts. But eventually he said, 'The reason why you were allowed to get away with it was that I didn't want to humiliate you before Daphne. I loved you, remember, and a man thinks twice before subjecting his loved one to embarrassment.'

She bit her lip.

'I'm sorry, Julius,' she murmured contritely. 'It was a strange thing,' she continued when he made no comment, 'but I gained the impression that you were reluctant to humiliate me. I think I've been very blind all this time.'

'Very, my love. You should have gained a clue when I told you, almost at the beginning, that until lately I had never seriously contemplated marriage.'

'That did register – some time afterwards,' she told him. 'But I thought you wanted me just for – for—'

'Well, I didn't! I wanted you for my companion and

friend, as well as my lover.'

Gale thrilled to these words, but just had to say,

'What would have happened if that pipe hadn't burst?'

He laughed with sheer amusement.

'How like a woman to think of that! It did burst, and so you were saved from a fate worse than death.'

She had to laugh then, in response to his continued amusement.

'I rather think you would have married me, just the same.'

'I rather think you're right,' he agreed, and drew her to his heart again.